Dead in a Pickup

Leah Norwood Mystery #3

B. L. Blair

Copyright © 2018 Brenda Blair
All rights reserved.

Cover art by Nicole Spence at Cover Shot Creations
http://www.covershotcreations.com

This is a work of fiction. Names, characters, places, and events either are the product of the author's imagination or are used fictitiously. Any resemblance to actual persons, business establishments, events, or locales is entirely coincidental.

ISBN: 1-944639-18-7
ISBN-13: 978-1-944639-18-1

CHAPTER 1

I found the body on April 12. It was a warm spring day, and I was surprised to see her sitting in the pickup, windows up, and engine turned off. It wasn't the best part of town, but the vehicle was in decent shape. I stared through the windshield. She appeared to be asleep, head back against the headrest, eyes closed. Then I saw the bruising around her neck so very reminiscent of my own. The tie lying on the seat next to her was familiar too.

#

"Nice tie," I said to the customer standing in front of me. It was a lovely shade of steel blue with gray stripes and went beautifully with the dark gray suit.

Of course, there isn't much that wouldn't look good on the man. Marcus Cantono was gorgeous. He was tall with jet-black hair and startling blue eyes. His face was classically handsome and his body—well—he had a great body. Typically when I saw him, he was dressed in jeans and a t-shirt that showed off his strong legs and broad shoulders, but he was on his way to work. In spite of the clothes, Marcus looked dangerous. He was a big man, not fat but muscular, and he radiated danger. Being part of a former drug-dealing clan added to the image. He was trying to steer the family to the legitimate side of the law. So far, he had only been marginally successful.

"Thanks, Leah," he said giving me a grin. My heartbeat sped up, my knees went weak, and a slight flush filled my face like a romance novel heroine. It was a natural reaction. One I couldn't have controlled even if I tried. Marcus's smile was something to behold. The problem was he knew it. His eyes roamed my face, and his grin widened.

"Stop it," I said sharply, glaring at him with narrowed eyes. He simply laughed.

An odd chain of events had made us friends. When Marcus returned to town to care for his aging mother, his family had been involved in a drug-dealing operation. Selling drugs was the family business, but Marcus had moved to California as a nineteen-year-old to escape that life.

I had accidentally intercepted a shipment of heroin and had come to the attention of his family. They had tried to intimidate me so I would stop asking questions. I'd been looking for a murderer—not a drug smuggler; although for a while, I thought they were the same. The encounter with the Cantonos had frightened me, but I wasn't about back down, and that had impressed Marcus. He had put the word out on the street that I was under his protection. A couple of weeks later, the whole drug operation had been taken down by the police, and some members of his family were arrested. Marcus swooped in to rescue the rest.

The younger members of the family were now working at the restaurant he had opened and trying to learn how to fit into mainstream society. The oldest Cantono brother, Damian, had been running the whole operation. He was out on bail and also trying to go straight. I had my doubts, but Marcus was determined to save his family, and I admired him for that.

I had been shocked when Marcus flirted with me and then asked me out. He was not the type of man I normally dated. I'm what most people would call average. Average height, average weight, average looks. Marcus was anything but average.

We'd gone on one date on New Year's Eve. He had kissed me at the stroke of midnight, and that was all it had taken for us to realize we were destined to be just friends. We didn't have that special chemistry, but the man's smile still made my toes curl.

"Tell your mother happy birthday," I said, handing him the bag with a packaged set of Rose in Bloom.

My store, Scents and Sensibility, sold lotions, soaps, and perfume in various fragrances. Rose in Bloom was one of our most popular. The packaged set came with all of the fragrance options. Marcus had purchased the exact same set for his mother at Christmas.

"You can tell her yourself," he said to me. "This Sunday evening we're having a private party at the restaurant. You're invited."

I smiled. The restaurant in question, Bella's, was one he had opened in late February. It was one of the finest in town, and the food was superb. He had an excellent chef and an attentive staff.

"Great. What time?"

"We're eating at six. Mama doesn't like to stay out late. Come by around five-thirty."

I'd met Marcus's mother, Arabella, on a couple of occasions. She hadn't liked me much the first time, but as soon as she realized I wasn't after her son, she became quite friendly. She liked me fine as a friend of the family. She just didn't want me marrying her youngest son. Arabella had said numerous times that Marcus needed a real Italian wife. In her mind, that meant someone who didn't work outside the home, was a great cook, and would worship the ground her son walked on. I didn't fit any of those categories.

Marcus didn't need that type of woman. He was already used to getting his way. One flash of his devastating smile and he usually got what he wanted. Marcus needed a woman who would stand up to him—someone who wasn't intimated by his good looks. Mama Arabella and I would have to disagree.

"I'll be there," I told him. "Now you need to leave. It's six, we're closing, and I've got a date."

"Ah. Our chief of police finally got a night off?"

Alexander Griggs was the police chief of our small city, Reed Hill, Texas. He had started his position in November. A few weeks later, I found the body of a woman in the dumpster behind my store. The woman in question had been shipping drugs for the Cantonos through the store she managed.

Isabel Meeks had not been a pleasant person, and few of us liked her. Because I had threatened her earlier in the day, I had been the lead suspect for a short time. It turned out the murder had nothing to do with the drugs or my dislike of Isabel. It had been the jealousy of an extremely troubled woman. Candace Hager had killed twice before trying to shoot a pregnant woman and strangle me. The murders had thrown our city into an uproar, but Griggs and I had worked together. We flirted a little and shared one steamy kiss. I had thought that meant something, but I didn't see him again until I found another body a couple of months later.

It had been a misunderstanding that had caused Griggs to disappear from my life. He had shown up at my apartment on New Year's Eve just in time to see me get into a car with Marcus. Believing I was involved with someone else, Griggs had removed himself from my life until the next murder. When he realized Marcus and I weren't dating, he warmed back up. Griggs and I saw each other fairly often. I would go to the police station to take him lunch or drop off one of my famous strawberry pies. He would stop by the store on his way to or from work or an interview. We just hadn't been on many official dates. Actually, we had been on four. Three others had to be canceled before they ever started. Two of the four dates had been interrupted by some police crisis mid-way through the evening, but the two dates we made it through to the end had been nice.

"Yes. He's off, and you need to go."

I pushed Marcus to the door. He laughed softly and wished me a good night. I locked the door behind him and headed to the back. My assistant manager, Emma Mayfield, was with another last minute shopper.

Normally, I didn't mind staying late. I loved my store, my employees, and my customers. Scents and Sensibility belonged to my two best friends and me. Gabriel Weston, Olivia

Graham, and I met in college. Gabe and Olivia married and moved back to Gabe's hometown. With no other prospects, I followed. I fell in love with Reed Hill but was working a dead-end job. Olivia was bored at hers, and Gabe had been handed the reins to his family's manufacturing business. One night of a little too much wine and our dream store was born. Olivia was a chemist. She mixed and designed our fragrances, Gabe's company produced them, and I sold them. For the last couple of years, we had turned a healthy profit, and we were all happy.

But I was anxious to leave. I hadn't seen Griggs for almost two weeks. During the shutdown of the Cantono's drug operation in December, the involvement of one of the local police captains had come to light. Raymond Hunter was still in prison, but his arrest had left a hole in the police department. Griggs had replaced him with an officer by the name of Megan Ross. She was smart, competent, and willing but lacked any real experience as a detective. Griggs had to spend a lot of time training her. She had been thrown into the deep end on her first case which had been the murder of a distant cousin of mine. That was the case that had brought Griggs back into my life.

Hunter had been the mastermind behind the drug operation, but he wasn't the only police officer involved. It had taken Griggs several months to weed out the rest which had left his department short-staffed.

If that had been the only thing in our way, Griggs and I would've found time to get together, but at the end of March, the flu arrived in town. It was late for a flu epidemic so everyone was surprised and unprepared. It started in the schools but swiftly spread. Emma, who had three young children, had to take off the whole first week of April. Usually, that wouldn't have been a problem as one of my other employees could have stepped in, but Myra, who was a retired teacher, had been helping out at the high school because so many were out sick. Our other option for help was Olivia, but two of her boys had also caught the flu. Kara and I were the only two left standing. Working a lot of hours didn't leave me much time for dating.

About the time, my employees returned to work, the flu made its way to the police and fire departments. Having emergency services short-handed was not anything anyone wanted. Griggs stepped in when Megan went down, and several other officers clocked a lot of overtime.

My phone rang as I walked into the backroom of the store. My heart sank when I saw it was Griggs. He wouldn't be calling unless he had to cancel. With a quiet sigh, I answered.

"I'm sorry," he said immediately. His deep, smoky voice sent a shiver down my spine—the good kind of shiver. I loved his voice.

"It's okay," I replied as I sat dejectedly in the chair behind my desk.

"No. It's not," he said sharply, "but I can't do anything about it. I found David in the bathroom throwing up."

David Reddish was the other captain on the Reed Hill force. He was in his late fifties, attractive, and had a crush on Myra. He was one of the most competent officers I had ever met as well as being a great guy.

"Flu?"

"Yep. He wasn't even going to tell me."

"He knows you need the time off."

"Yeah, but…"

"It's okay. I understand."

"I'm really sorry, Leah."

"I know."

"Listen, Megan is supposed to be back tomorrow. I'll brief her in the morning, and then we can grab lunch. Do you think you could get the afternoon off? We can make a day of it."

I leaned back in the chair with a silly look on my face. "I think I can arrange that."

"Great." I could hear the smile in his voice. "I'll call you in the morning."

We chatted a few more minutes before he was called away. I had just gotten off the phone when Emma came in.

"What are you still doing here?" she exclaimed. "Go. I'll

lock up."

"No need," I replied. "He had to cancel."

"Oh, no. Not again."

"David has the flu."

Emma's eyes flew open wide. A small smile started forming on her face and quickly became a huge grin.

"Do you think he got it from Myra?" she asked.

The two of us had been trying to get Myra and David together for a couple of months. Myra had a bad relationship in her past. Her ex-husband, Leon, had been abusive, and she was skittish. David was making headway, but her ex had recently resurfaced which brought back a lot of unpleasant memories. He had been working with the man who had killed my distant cousin. Leon had held Myra and the oldest Weston boy hostage to make me cooperate. Myra had hit him over the head with a pitchfork. I think that did more for her relationship with David than anything. By defending herself and Aaron, she had freed herself from Leon's influence. She had accepted a couple of David's invitations to dinner.

"I don't think Myra had the flu," I said with a laugh.

"No," Emma agreed, "but she might be a carrier. She was around all those kids. I'm going to assume he contracted it because he was close to her. It's much more romantic that way."

"The flu's not romantic."

"No, but how he caught it could be."

"True," I said with a sigh. "It would be nice to be close enough to catch the flu."

"Sorry about your date. The two of you have had the worst luck."

"I know, but he said Megan will be back tomorrow. He's going to meet me for lunch, and we're going to spend the day together. You and Kara will be on your own tomorrow afternoon."

"Not a problem. Why don't you take the whole day off? Aren't you meeting Tracy tomorrow morning?"

Tracy Hamilton was my real estate agent. I was in the

market for a house. My search had been put on hold with everything that had been going on, but she had called me earlier in the day stating she had found a great deal.

"I am, but it's early. We're meeting at eight. I should have plenty of time to view the house and still get here before we open."

"Well, good luck."

"Thanks. Now let's go home."

CHAPTER 2

The house was...nice. It had a long porch and several windows. The roof was a little odd as it had painted strips of pale pink and white, but it blended with the light paint on the rest of the house, and the landscaping was lovely. There was a huge flower bed along and around the side of the house. It was full of plants and flowers, and there were two medium sized trees in the yard. The house was certainly the best one in the neighborhood.

And I hated it.

Hated was probably too strong a word. How can someone hate a house? But it wasn't my dream home. Of course, my dream home had been sold out from under me when I wasn't looking. That house, a small Cape Cod style home, had gone on the market in late February and sold two days later. It was located in the same area as my current apartment. The house faced our city park, and homes in that area were seldom up for sale. I'd called Tracy the minute I saw it was available. She contacted the other agent who already had another offer. The house had been sold before I could even look at it, and I was heartbroken.

After that, I had put the search for a new home temporarily on hold. I'd planned to wait a couple of weeks before looking again, but with everything that happened at work and with Griggs, those two weeks turned into a month. I had kept an eye on the Cape Cod home. The For Sale sign came down, but no one moved in. I was hoping the sale would fall through, and I would be able to sweep in and claim it. After six weeks, I finally came to the conclusion the house was lost to me.

When Tracy called to ask if I was ever going to start looking again, I said yes. Now I was searching for another dream home, and I could already tell this one wasn't it.

My phone rang, startling me out of my musings. Looking at the screen, I suppressed a sigh. Tracy was determined to get me into a home as soon as possible. Her aggressiveness worried me.

"Hi, Tracy."

"Leah, I'm on my way. There was an accident on the freeway. I'm still in the backup but almost to the next exit. I should be there in about ten minutes."

"Okay."

"Leah," she said. "I know you had your heart set on the house on Park Lane, but this one's a steal. It's in great shape. The owner is desperate to sell. It's close to your work, and it's lower than your budget."

All good things. All the things I had hoped to find.

"I know. It looks nice."

"Take a look around. Go into the backyard. It's a good size. Harry will love it."

I glanced at the dog sitting in the passenger seat of my car. Harry was a light brown color and had a lot of fur, hence his name. I didn't name him. Oliva's eight-year-old son did. Eric liked the play on words so my hairy dog became Harry.

"I'll look around, but there's someone else here."

"Who?" Tracy asked sharply.

"I don't know. There's a pickup parked in front of the house, and someone's sitting inside."

"Hmm. No one else is showing the house today. I checked."

"Well, maybe they're waiting for someone across the street or something."

Tracy agreed and hung up, vowing to meet me as soon as she could. I got out of my four-month-old car. In December,

I'd been run off the road by Candace the first time she tried to kill me. It was after she killed Isabel, but before she killed Anthony Thorpe. It was several days later before she tried to strangle me. She was now in jail and headed for institutional treatment, and I had a new car. It sounds funny, but it wasn't.

My last car had been an awful bright fuchsia but reliable. The odd color had made it almost impossible for the dealer to sell so I had taken the great deal that was offered. It had been a good car and completely paid off, but after the wreck, I received a check from the insurance company and decided to purchase a new car. I splurged. This one was a normal shade of gray, but it was flashier and faster than my last car. It had a 6-cylinder engine. I didn't know what that meant. Cars weren't my thing, but Gabe had been excited about it and assured me it would have a little get-up-and-go.

Harry jumped out after me and danced around a little. He's still a young dog and big. The vet estimated he was about two and thought he was a mixture of collie, sheepdog, and some other large breed. He had a lot of energy but had turned out to be a great pet. Loyal and protective. He generally went to work with me each day. Harry stayed in the back room and was babied by all my employees and some of my customers. I was able to spend my breaks with him and take him for walks during the day. On the same day I acquired Harry, I had found a sick cat. Pandora moved in and now ruled our home. Taking Harry to work with me gave her a break from the overeager dog. It worked well for all of us.

As we headed toward the house, I glanced at the pickup. The woman inside didn't move. I could tell it was a woman by her hair and the shape of her face. She appeared to be asleep. Shrugging, I led Harry up the sidewalk to the porch. The porch was big enough for a couple of chairs. I could picture myself sitting outside on a cool spring or fall evening reading a book or watching the birds in the trees.

The neighborhood was an older one. Most of the houses were in poor shape, but the area was near a major street and housing was at a premium in Reed Hill. If a developer was smart, they would buy the houses and renovate them. It wouldn't take much for the neighborhood to become the newest hot spot. If I could get in before everyone else, I would have equity in my home far quicker than normal.

As we walked toward the back, I started to get a little excited. It was obvious the house was in good shape. The porch was smooth and even. I didn't see any cracks in the siding or foundation. The house had been recently painted, and the air conditioning unit was large and clean. A wooden fence that looked new surrounded the backyard.

I opened the gate to the backyard, and Harry rushed in. I let the leash go and watched as he raced around. As Tracy had said, it was a good size. There was plenty of room for the dog to roam, and there was a small porch at the back door. I walked around the yard for a few minutes inspecting the fence before peering through the windows. I couldn't see much so I called for Harry and returned to the front of the house.

Tracy still hadn't arrived so I sat on the top step of the porch. Harry sniffed around the bushes a few minutes before settling down next to me. A car sped by revving its engine. There were two young men inside. One of them shot me the finger as they passed. I frowned and rolled my eyes. It wasn't pleasant, but I had my Glock in my purse, and it was daylight. I could defend myself if they decided to challenge me. I wasn't worried. The car continued down the road and turned the corner. Other than that, the neighborhood was quiet. I could hear a dog barking a few houses away, but there was no one outside.

I looked at the house across the street. The grass was overgrown, and there were several cars parked in the driveway. The house next to it had almost no grass, and one of the windows was boarded up. I was starting to lose the little bit of excitement I had when looking at the house. It was nice and in good shape, but the area was a little scary.

I needed to ask someone impartial about the neighborhood. Tracy was a new agent, and I had been stringing her along for a while. I had a feeling she was going to push me into a home to get me off her books. I didn't want to live somewhere that wasn't safe.

Glancing at the pickup again, I wondered if the woman would know anything. If she was waiting for someone who lived in the area, she might be familiar with the residents. She still hadn't moved, and I was getting a little worried. It was a warm spring day, and I was surprised she was sitting in the cab with the windows up and the engine turned off.

Before I could decide whether to approach her, my phone rang. Thinking it was Tracy, I answered without checking. I was surprised to hear Griggs on the line.

"Good morning," he said when I answered.

"Hi," I replied with a smile. "Please don't tell me you can't make lunch."

"Are you kidding me?" he said, humor lining his voice. "I think I'd get run out of town if I canceled on you again."

"Oh, I doubt that."

"You weren't at the council meeting or at the gym."

"What do you mean?"

"Gabe made a very pointed comment at the city council meeting the other night about not showing for our double date."

As one of the leading employers in town, Gabe sat on the city council. He had been instrumental in hiring Griggs as our police chief, and he and Griggs had become friends. Gabe, Olivia, Griggs, and I had planned to meet at the movies on Saturday. It was one of the times Griggs had to cancel. Gabe understood this. He was simply giving Griggs a hard time.

"He had to know you couldn't help it," I said.

"Sure. As a council member and city leader, he understands and supports my dedication to the job. But as your friend, he's not happy."

I could still hear the humor in Griggs's voice so I didn't apologize for Gabe's behavior. My friends could be protective.

"Of course, Cantono wasn't as understanding."

"Marcus?"

"Yes. Marcus. When I saw him at the gym this morning, he

asked how our date went. He wasn't pleased when I told him I had to cancel. I think he might've threatened my life."

I laughed. Marcus and Griggs had gotten off on the wrong foot. Griggs being law enforcement and Marcus being part of a law-breaking family hadn't helped. They now seemed to have reached an understanding. Not exactly friends, but no longer enemies.

"I'm sure he didn't mean it," I said. "You must've gotten to the gym early."

"Yeah. I got a decent night's sleep as it was quiet at the station. No domestic calls, no accidents, and especially no murders. I had to sleep on the couch in my office, but I wasn't disturbed. I think that may be what pissed off Cantono. He didn't look like he had slept at all."

"That's odd. I saw him at the store yesterday. He didn't mention any late plans. Just going to Bella's to help out. Maybe he didn't sleep well and went to the gym early to wear himself out so he could sleep tonight."

"Maybe. He certainly looked tired, but enough about him. What are you doing?"

"I'm sitting on the porch of a house waiting for my real estate agent to arrive so she can show it to me. Do you know anything about an accident on the freeway?"

There was a short pause. "We heard about it, but it's being handled by the state troopers. They didn't ask for any assistance so it can't be that bad."

"Probably a fender-bender that backed up traffic. Tracy said she was almost to the exit. Hopefully, she'll be here soon."

Another pause. "You're looking for a house?"

He sounded surprised. It had been my plan to purchase a house for years. I had been saving for a down payment that would allow me to have a reasonable monthly mortgage. We had paid off all our business loans, and the store was doing well. Buying a house had been such a big part of my life for a while now that I didn't realize until that moment I had never mentioned it to Griggs. In some ways, it felt like we'd been dating forever, but in reality, we still barely knew each other. I took a few minutes to tell him about my plans.

"I just bought a house myself," he said. "I thought I could show it to you today."

"I'd love to see it."

"Great. I'll meet you at the store around one."

I agreed, and we said goodbye. I was starting to get worried about Tracy. The ten minutes had stretched to thirty, and she still wasn't anywhere in sight. I looked up and down the street. There was no traffic. Cars were parked along the curbs, but nothing was moving. It was a little eerie.

The woman in the pickup still hadn't moved. I rose from the porch and walked toward her. The pickup was old, but it was in decent shape. It looked like something from the fifties or sixties with a smaller cab and bed. The closer I got, the more concerned I became. She was so still. A knot formed in my stomach as I edged nearer.

The woman appeared to be asleep, head back against the headrest, eyes closed, but I knew she wasn't asleep. I stared through the windshield and saw the bruising around her neck so very reminiscent of my own. Unfortunately, the tie lying on the seat next to her was familiar too.

Tracy pulled up behind my car as I was calling 911. It was too late for the woman inside, but I knew a crime scene when I saw one. The one thought that kept running through my head was what was Marcus's tie doing on the seat of a dead woman's pickup?

CHAPTER 3

The police arrived quickly. Tracy had bolted into the house as soon as I mentioned the dead woman. She didn't see the body but turned a little green when she rushed through the door. I stayed outside waiting for the authorities. I was shaken up as well. Finding someone dead isn't pleasant, but this was the fifth body I had found in four months. You never get used to it, but it didn't affect me as much as it did the first time.

Most of the officers on the Reed Hill Police Department knew me. Some of them because we lived in the same town but many because I hung around with Griggs and David Reddish. There were twenty-five patrol officers currently on the force. Griggs was hoping to hire a few more. They worked in pairs, but with the odd number, there was always one driving solo. That was the case with Benjie Bottoms.

I didn't know Benjie well, having spoken to him only a couple of times. He used to be teamed up with Megan Ross before her promotion. He was a middle-aged man with a slightly round body. Short and squat was the best description. His hair was a dusty brown, and he had a sweet smile. Although older than Megan, I had never seen any resentment toward her from Benjie which made me like him even more.

"Morning Ms. Norwood," he said to me as he got out of the car.

"Morning."

"What've we got?"

"There's a dead woman in the pickup."

"You sure she's dead?" he asked.

I shrugged. "I didn't check her pulse or anything, but she hasn't moved since I got here. She has bruises around her neck, and she doesn't look like she's breathing."

He held up one finger indicating he wanted me to wait. He walked over to the pickup pulling on rubber gloves. Benjie probably didn't have much experience with murder victims, but this wasn't his first dead body. The murder rate in Reed Hill wasn't high. It was my bad luck to keep discovering the few that did occur. Benjie moved cautiously. Slowly, he opened the door being careful that nothing fell out before reaching in to check for a pulse. Shaking his head, he turned back to me as two other cars pulled up to the house.

The first was a dark blue SUV. I once teased Griggs that he had a soccer mom car. He didn't find that as funny as I did and told me curtly it was the perfect car for surveillance. When he got out, his intense green eyes immediately cut to me.

Alexander Griggs was breathtaking—not gorgeous or handsome like Marcus, but there was a power about him that drew the eye. He wasn't exceptionally tall, standing about five eleven, but he had long smooth strides that ate up space. His shoulders were broad and his hips narrow, and there wasn't an ounce of fat on his hard, lean body. He wore his dark hair cut short, military style. His face was attractive in a timeless way with a small indentation on the right side of his mouth that tried extremely hard to be a dimple. I loved that tiny dimple.

Once he determined I wasn't injured, he headed straight for Benjie and the pickup. I had to hold Harry back. He loved Griggs and wanted to greet him. Harry actually loved anyone who played with him. The dog wanted to run but sat on my command.

The second car was a standard police-issued sedan. The driver was Megan Ross. Megan was competent, serious, and pretty. She used to try to hide the pretty behind a severe hairstyle and no makeup. As the sole female on the police force at the time, she had been trying to be taken seriously.

Since her promotion to captain, I was happy to notice she had loosened up. She dressed sharp and professional, but her clothes were feminine. The jacket fit her well, and she wore a touch of makeup. She never looked my way, instead hurried to catch up with Griggs.

The three police officers conferred and began taking pictures. Griggs opened the door of the pickup and leaned in. He appeared to be searching for something. When he stood back up, he held the tie from the tip of his finger. Megan stiffened, her head jerking back. Her eyes darted to me for just a moment before she straightened her shoulders. I frowned at her reaction.

Pulling an evidence bag from her pocket, she held it open for Griggs. He placed the tie in the bag and said something to Megan. She shook her head and whispered something back. Griggs nodded once.

With a sinking feeling, I returned to the porch. Harry trailed behind me and settled at my feet with an eye on all the activity. Megan had recognized the tie. It was the only explanation for her reaction. In a way, I was relieved. I wouldn't have to mention I had seen the exact same tie on Marcus. On the other hand, I was worried because I had seen the exact same tie on Marcus. Was it his or did someone else have an identical tie?

"I don't suppose you want to look at the house," Tracy said as she stepped out onto the porch.

I laughed humorlessly. The house was the least of my concerns. Tracy sat down next to me and stared at the commotion around the pickup. Her face grew grim.

"No one's going to want to look at this house," she muttered.

"I wouldn't bet on that. The police will want to search it."

"That wasn't what I meant."

"I know," I replied, "but don't look so glum. There're people who will be attracted to the morbid aspect of someone dying here. Besides, she wasn't killed in the house. At least, I don't think she was."

"How long do you think this is going to take? I've got

another appointment." She didn't wait for me to answer before continuing. "Do you think I need to stay? I didn't find her, and I don't know anything."

I glanced at her. Tracy and I weren't friends. I had engaged her because of a recommendation from a customer. Marie had been a longtime supporter of Scents and Sensibility. Tracy was her cousin, and Marie had asked me to hire her. I didn't know any other agents, and she seemed competent, but the longer I was around her, the less I liked her.

"I don't know," I replied. "You could ask them."

Tracy stood, smoothed out her clothes, and started toward the officers. She was halfway across the yard when they noticed her. I hid a smile when I saw the look on Megan's face. I had seen that look before, and things didn't bode well for Tracy.

Megan stopped her before she got close to the pickup. The two of them had a terse conversation. Tracy huffed and returned to the porch. Both Megan and Griggs followed her.

"Now, Ms. Hamilton," Megan said. "What time did you arrive?"

I listened absently as Megan interviewed Tracy whose answers were brief and angry. Megan was calm and methodical while Tracy's answers grew shriller. Griggs greeted Harry and sat on the steps beside me.

"Are you all right?" he asked softly.

Rubbing my hands up and down my arms, I nodded. "Who is she…was she?"

"Brandy Perez. Does that ring a bell?"

"No. Does she live around here?"

"Next door."

Startled, I looked at him and then the house next door. It wasn't in great shape, but it was one of the few on the street that looked like someone was trying to keep up. The yard was mowed and tidy. All the windows were intact, and the front door closed properly. There was a short driveway; however, it looked like it was being repaired as it was torn up near the curb. That explained why the pickup was parked in front of the neighbor's house, but it didn't explain why she was still in it.

"Why didn't anyone check on her? Report it? I've been here since a little before eight. It's a weekday. Kids had to be going to school. People to work. Why didn't anyone see her before now?"

"Leah," Griggs said. "Look around. What's missing?"

I studied the scene. The pickup was still in place. All our cars lined the street. Benjie's police cruiser still had its lights flashing although the sirens were off. What was missing? People. Normally by now, a crowd would have gathered, but there was no one.

"Where is everyone?"

"Hiding. Staying low. This area of town is known for illegal activities. They don't like the police. I'm surprised you're looking at a home here."

"I didn't know anything about the neighborhood. The house is in good shape, and it's a great deal. Tracy thought it fit most of my requirements."

"You need to add safe neighborhood to your list of requirements."

"I thought that was a given," I muttered softly.

Megan had finished with Tracy who huffed one last time and stalked away. We watched her stomp to her car and slam the door behind her before trying to maneuver around all the cars in the street. Her show of indignation lost some of its potency when she had to creep slowly between Benjie's car and mine.

Shaking her head, Megan walked over to us. She glanced at Griggs questioningly. He nodded so she turned to me.

"Tell me what happened."

Megan and Griggs were silent while I told them everything I had done since I arrived that morning. I had been through enough interviews that little prompting was needed.

"So you didn't see anyone when you arrived?"

"No. I haven't seen anyone at all except for the car that drove by."

"What type of car?"

"Um, black?"

Beside me, Griggs snorted. As I mentioned, I don't know anything about cars. I have trouble remembering the make and model of my own. I would never have recognized the type of car belonging to someone else.

"Was it two or four doors?" Megan asked patiently.

"Oh. Two."

She continued to ask me questions about the car. With her guidance, she got a decent description. She and Griggs even narrowed down the make to one or two options.

"Okay," Megan continued. "What about the two men? Would you recognize either of them?"

"Not the driver. I didn't see him very well, but the passenger gave me a friendly wave." I raised one hand and wiggled my middle finger. "I got a pretty good look at his face."

I gave Megan a general description of the one I saw. She said they would check to see who lived in or frequented the neighborhood and perhaps have me look at a few mugshots. She jotted down a few notes. There was a long pause. Megan took a deep breath and looked at Griggs.

"I'd like to speak with Leah alone," she said.

"Why?" he asked softly.

Megan looked at me and then back at him. Before she could speak, I reached out and placed a hand on his leg. Griggs turned to me. I gave him a tight smile.

"Why don't you go see what Benjie is doing?"

His face closed, his eyes narrowed, and his lips flattened into a straight line, but he didn't say a word. He rose and walked away. Once he was out of hearing range, Megan took his place on the steps beside me. She pulled out the evidence bag with the steel blue tie. She placed it on her lap and smoothed it out.

"Do you recognize this?"

I didn't answer right away. I wasn't sure what she was wanting, and I didn't want to lie. Marcus Cantono was a dangerous man. There was no doubt in my mind he would kill to protect those he loved. He had even offered to make sure that Candace had an "accident" in prison for me. Although I wasn't afraid of him, he could be a scary man. However, I knew he had not murdered Brandy Perez. He never would've been stupid enough to leave behind anything that would lead the police to him.

"I've seen a tie that looks like that one recently," I told Megan carefully. "I can't say it was that tie."

"Where did you see it?"

"At my store."

Megan drew in another deep breath. "Who was wearing it?"

"Why did you ask to speak with me alone?"

She gave me a hard stare. It was effective. I squirmed a little. "Who was wearing the tie, Ms. Norwood?"

"Marcus Cantono."

She nodded and started to rise. I grabbed her arm and pulled her back down. Her eyes tightened. She looked at me and then pointedly looked at my hand on her arm. I quickly released her. I liked Megan a lot, but I didn't want to be on her bad side.

"How did you recognize the tie?" I asked her.

A slight frown crossed her face. She looked away. Staring down, she folded the evidence bag in half and smoothed out her pant leg. She looked up but didn't look at me.

"I also saw Marc—Mr. Cantono wearing it yesterday."

"You saw Marcus? Where?" I demanded. The look she gave me wasn't pretty, but I was beyond caring. She was hiding something, and my curiosity was aroused. "Hey, you're the one who wanted to speak to me alone. I think I have a right to know."

She sighed and looked over at Griggs. "I picked up some food from Bella's last night. I saw Mr. Cantono there."

"So why did you ask me about the tie?"

"It was dark. The to-go pickup area is in the bar. The lighting in there is low. I wanted to be sure..."

"If you told Griggs the tie belonged to Marcus, he would have you arrest him."

What she said made sense if she was trying to protect

Marcus. What I didn't know was why. Why was a police captain trying to protect a Cantono?

"The tie's not enough to arrest him, but we'll have to question him." She stood abruptly. "Thank you for your statement. We'll be in touch if we have any other questions. You may go."

With that, she walked away. I gathered Harry and headed to my car. The medical examiner had arrived, and they were loading Brandy onto a stretcher. A couple of other officers were dusting for prints and searching the truck. Griggs gave me a nod but didn't come over.

I got into the car and watched the activity for a moment. Megan had pulled Griggs aside and was talking earnestly to him with the evidence bag in her hand. Griggs was shaking his head and gesturing angrily. I drove away thinking things really did not look good for Marcus.

CHAPTER 4

Instead of driving to work, I placed a call to Marcus. It went directly to voice mail so I sent a text. No response. It didn't even show as delivered which meant he had either turned off his phone or was out of range. I wanted to warn him, but it didn't seem right to simply leave a message about a dead body so I turned the car west.

Reed Hill was located north of Dallas. There was a main highway running through town that led south into Dallas and north into Oklahoma. Scattered along the highway were restaurants, hotels, shopping centers, and gas stations. It was a busy area, and Bella's Fine Italian Restaurant was just off the highway. The location was perfect as it attracted both the locals and those driving through town. It was a smart move by Marcus. The restaurant had been open a couple of months, and it was doing well.

Bella's didn't open until eleven, but Marcus didn't work regular hours. He hired a competent manager and staff. He kept an eye on things but only stopped by the restaurant once a day or to help out if someone was late or unable to come into work. He was opening a second location in McKinney, a city about twenty minutes south of Reed Hill, which was taking up most of his time.

I didn't expect to find Marcus at Bella's, but it was a place to start. One of his employees or family members might know how to reach him. There were no cars in the parking lot when

I arrived. I parked and pulled out my phone. Still no response from Marcus. My second call also went directly to voice mail. I was now worried enough to leave a message. The longer I waited, the more likely the police would get to him first.

"Hey, Marcus. It's Leah. Listen, call me as soon as you get this message. Before you speak to anyone else if you can. Something happened. I, uh, I found another body. A woman named Brandy Perez. It looked like she had been strangled with a tie...with...your tie...Call me."

Biting my lip, I stared at the building willing one of the staff to arrive so I could question them. I really wanted to find Marcus.

When I first learned about the Cantono family, they were living in Mayville. Damian owned a small house where they sold drugs, and Arabella lived next door. I still didn't know how much Arabella knew about the drug operation, but Marcus moved her into his house in a new subdivision in Reed Hill. That had lasted about a month. Arabella wanted her own home so Marcus purchased her a smaller house nearby. The problem was I didn't know the address of either one of them.

For a time, Marcus had Damian's two sons working for him. Mike seemed to be doing okay. He was even taking a couple of classes at the community college. The other nephew, Ricky, was a different story. He hadn't gotten in any trouble with the law, but he wasn't trying very hard to hold down a job. Marcus had to fire him from the restaurant because he wouldn't show up on time for his shift—if he showed up at all. Last I knew, Ricky was living with his girlfriend in the Harbor Trailer Park. Ricky didn't like me, but if I could find him, he might tell me how to find Marcus.

Damian Cantono had been released on bail in March. He was awaiting trial for the drug-smuggling operation. Marcus wouldn't say, but I was pretty sure he, Marcus, paid the bond. Damian was also working at the restaurant part-time. He hadn't spoken to me the two times I saw him, but he seemed to be taking his new duties seriously. I had no idea where he was living, and he liked me even less than Ricky did. Even if I could track him down, I didn't think he would tell me where Marcus lived.

After waiting another ten minutes, a car pulled into the parking lot. I immediately knew it wasn't Marcus. He drove a black, sporty car. This was a silver pickup. The driver was the assistant manager whose name I couldn't remember. He gave me an odd look when he got out of the car. I smiled and rolled down the window.

"Hi. I'm looking for Marcus. Have you heard from him?"

"No."

"Are you expecting him today?"

The man shrugged. "He usually stops by, but I can't say I'm expecting him."

"If he does, will you please tell him to call me?"

"Uh, yeah, sure." He paused, looked around the parking lot, and back at me. "Are you just going to sit here and wait for him?"

"No. Of course not," I said with a false laugh. The thought had crossed my mind, but with the man looking at me as if I was crazy, I decided against it. "Is Damian working today?"

"Not until tonight. You looking for him too?"

"No," I huffed. "Please let Marcus know I'm looking for him if you see him."

"Okay," he replied before shaking his head and walking to the back door.

I quickly put my car into drive and left. I already had a reputation as a busybody and snoop. I didn't need to add crazy to the list. With no other idea of where to look for Marcus, I headed into work.

My store, Scents and Sensibility, was located in downtown Reed Hill. The downtown area was a historic district with a beautiful old courthouse. The courthouse was used for events and meetings as we had a modern building for most of the legal proceedings. The square was now filled with antique stores, restaurants, and specialty shops like mine.

Most of the stores in the area were open from ten a.m. to six p.m. Monday through Saturday. We got a lot of business on

Saturday from all the neighboring towns, but during the week, it was mostly locals. I pulled into a parking space behind the store just after ten-thirty. I got Harry settled in the back room before going into the store itself. There were no customers, but both Emma and my other full-time employee, Kara Bennett, were there.

"I heard you found another body," Kara said dryly.

Kara was younger than my other employees. Emma and I were about the same age, and Myra was in her fifties, but Kara was twenty-three. She was a lovely woman with dark, flawless skin and a slightly crooked smile. She'd been working for me for about two years. I found her reliable and capable, but quiet. She wasn't shy, just introverted. We didn't have a lot in common, but I enjoyed her dry sense of humor. She had recently gotten engaged, and I was worried I might lose her as an employee.

"How did you already hear about that?" I asked.

"Marie was standing at the door when I opened," Emma said. "You just missed her."

Marie had been coming to our store a couple of times a month since we opened for business. She knew both Emma and I liked to arrive early to check everything before we opened for the day. Because she was such a loyal customer, we sometimes let her in before ten.

"She was on the phone with Tracy," Emma continued. I grimaced, but Emma grinned. "Marie said she appreciates that you hired Tracy based on her recommendation, but her new recommendation is to fire her."

"Really?" I asked somewhat startled.

Emma nodded. "She told me she only asked you to work with Tracy because her mother asked her to help Tracy find some customers. According to Marie, Tracy isn't doing well in the real estate business."

"I'm not surprised. She isn't very personable."

"I don't think Marie thinks so either. Tracy blamed Marie for referring her to you. She thinks you are odd and maybe dangerous."

"Dangerous?" I squeaked.

"Apparently, you keep getting involved with murders."

"She's the one who recommended the house!"

"I don't think you have to worry about her anymore," Emma said. "Now tell us what happened."

Once again, I relayed the events of that morning. I would be telling the story multiple times over the next few days. Gabe and Olivia would want to hear it as would many of my other friends and my customers. Emma and Kara listened attentively and peppered me with questions.

It wasn't long before people started stopping by the store—both customers and others who worked in the area. I got phone calls from Gabe, Olivia, and a few friends. By lunch time, I had told the story so many times I was sick of it. The one person I hadn't heard from was Marcus.

Griggs showed up for our lunch date. I hadn't been certain he would, but he'd called to reassure me he would be there. He was still dressed in his work clothes which was a business suit. Like Marcus, Griggs filled it out nicely. He favored gray suits with plain ties. The one he was wearing was a soft pewter.

"I won't be able to take the whole afternoon off like I'd hoped," he said when we were seated at Nora's Bakery.

Nora's was a staple in my diet. It was located next door to Scents and Sensibility so I ate there several times a week. I probably would have done so because it was convenient, but the food was awfully good too. They served breakfast and lunch daily as well as an afternoon tea twice a week. It had a quaint and old-fashioned feel. They also had the most delicious strawberry scones I had ever tasted.

I loved strawberries. I loved the taste, the look, the smell of them. The first fragrance Olivia had created for our store was Leah's Strawberry Essence. I loved it. It's not sickeningly sweet. Instead, it was the smell of freshly picked strawberries, and I wore it every day.

"I understand," I said taking a bite of my sandwich. It wasn't the most romantic meal, but it was pretty typical for the two of us. "I know the murder is going to take up your time."

Griggs lowered his head and shot me a look. "I can't talk to you about it."

"Like I'm not going to find out. You might as well tell me. You know how gossip flies through this place." He shook his head. "At least tell me this. Have you spoken with Marcus?"

"No. Have you?"

"No," I said, glancing at my phone. "He hasn't returned my call."

"We haven't been able to reach him either."

"He's not at his house?"

Griggs sighed and laid his sandwich down on the plate. "I thought this was supposed to be a date. You know, just the two of us. Not my job. Not a murder."

I tilted my head. "Look around you, Alex. We're in a bakery being watched by everyone in here. People are texting their friends, and I'm sure more people will show up soon. Besides, isn't that typical for the two of us?"

"Unfortunately."

"I'm worried about Marcus, but if you don't want to talk about him, pick another subject."

"Fine," Griggs said sharply. "He's not answering any phone number we have for him. He's not at his house, the restaurant, or his mother's. She said he had a meeting in McKinney with a contractor, but she didn't know who and neither does anyone else. And on the subject of Cantono, were you going to tell me the tie was his?"

"I didn't know the tie was his. Do you?"

There couldn't have been enough time to prove the tie belonged to Marcus. If the police hadn't spoken with him, the only way to be sure would be some type of DNA test or fingerprints in the pickup. I didn't know how long something like that would take, but there was no way Griggs had the results yet.

"Both you and Ross stated he was wearing a tie that matches the one we found at the crime scene."

"That doesn't mean it's his."

"Leah," Griggs said exasperated. "Why are you defending

him? Remember his wife."

Marcus's wife, Lucy, had drowned in the family pool in California. Neighbors had heard the two of them arguing right before she died and saw him drive away. When he returned the next morning, he found her in the pool. There had been a bump on the back of her head indicating she had hit a table or chair before falling in. Marcus had been questioned several times by the police because the time of death had been set as the same hour of the argument. Lucy's blood alcohol level had been exceedingly high, and it was finally ruled an accidental death. She had wandered out to the pool after Marcus left, slipped, hit her head, and drowned. Marcus had been cleared but mostly for lack of evidence, not because they believed he was innocent.

"I don't believe he killed his wife," I said. "And neither do you."

Griggs started to reply, but I interrupted him. "Besides, that proves my point. Nothing tied him to her death. Why would he be stupid enough to leave evidence behind for this one?"

"Then where is he? Why can't we find him?"

"I don't know. I just…" My phone buzzed, and I quickly picked it up. "Where are you?"

"I'm heading to the police station now," Marcus replied. "You can tell your boyfriend I'll meet him there."

"Marcus…" I stopped as I was talking to dead air. I looked at Griggs. "He's on his way to the station. He said he would meet you there."

Griggs rose from his chair, and turned to the door. He stopped and turned back looking at me. He gave me a sad smile. "I guess this is us, isn't it?"

My stomach dropped. I really liked Griggs. Our relationship had gotten off to a rocky start and never gained any momentum, but I was already half in love with him. I didn't want to lose that before it even started.

"Is that a bad thing?" I whispered.

He walked over to me, leaned down, and gave me a soft kiss. "No, it's not a bad thing. Just not what I was expecting. I guess I need to readjust my expectations."

He was gone before I could reply, but I released a relieved breath. I was still sitting there staring after him when Juliet stopped by the table.

Juliet was the manager of Nora's. She was a blunt, practical woman who wasn't friendly with the other merchants. I didn't interact with her often, but she was a great baker, and I happily ate the wonderful things she produced.

"You want me to box that up?" she asked. She was actually pretty good with customers. She just didn't want to associate with anyone outside of work.

"What?" I asked.

"The chief's lunch. Do you want me to box it up?"

I glanced at Griggs's plate. He had eaten about a third of his sandwich and almost none of the potato salad. A smile spread across my face. A man needs to eat.

"Yes, please. I'll be happy to take it to him."

CHAPTER 5

My trip to the police station did not go well. I got past the receptionist at the front desk. She knew me and waved me in. Carrying the Styrofoam box from Nora's was a clue I was dropping off lunch. Griggs wasn't in his office and neither was Megan Ross. One of the patrol officers told me they were interviewing Marcus. I was just settling down to wait when Griggs returned, thanked me for lunch, and escorted me from the building.

"Go home, Leah," he said firmly.

"Wait. How is Marcus?"

"He's fine." Griggs studied me. "Is there more to your relationship with him than I know?"

"What!? No!"

"No? You seem overly concerned about him."

"We're friends. You know that."

"Maybe you want more?"

"Why are you saying that? I told you we only went out once."

Griggs hadn't asked me much about my date with Marcus, but it was why he hadn't pursued a relationship with me sooner. Why he was bringing it up now?

"Look, Alex. Marcus and I are friends. Yes, he's a handsome man, but there's nothing sexual between us."

"I believe you think that, but I'm not sure it's true." He gave me a slight smile and quietly shut my car door before walking away.

Stunned, I watched him for a moment. Where had that come from? Was he truly worried about my relationship with Marcus? I didn't know how to fix something I didn't think was a problem.

As Griggs walked up the stairs to the station, he was stopped by a man dressed in an expensive suit. Griggs's back stiffened, and his face went blank. He reluctantly shook hands. The man was in his early fifties. He was a little taller than Griggs and had shiny brown hair. It took me a little while to place him, and when I did, I wasn't sure whether to be relieved or worried.

Charles Bunting was one of the top criminal attorneys in the state. He had an excellent reputation and a thriving practice. I was somewhat surprised to see him. The Cantono family was not his usual type of client. Marcus must have pulled some strings or thrown a lot of money his way.

I sent Marcus a text. *Did you hire Charles Bunting?*

This time the text showed delivered. I waited, hoping he would be able to respond. It took a few minutes, but my phone finally buzzed.

Yes. The cavalry has arrived. You can go now.

Shaking my head, I wondered how he knew I was there. With no other option, I returned to the store, picked up Harry, and headed home. I had the whole afternoon free, and I knew exactly how I was going to spend it.

My apartment complex was a few minutes from downtown. I lived in one of the units facing Ash Street. Most of the buildings contained four separate apartments. Two on the ground floor and two above them. I had one of the apartments on the second floor. The other upstairs apartment was currently occupied by a middle-aged, divorced, businessman. I didn't know what Patrick actually did for a living, but he traveled a lot. He was polite and always let me know when he was going to be gone for longer than one night. Other than that, we barely spoke to one another. Mr. Brooks lived in the apartment below Patrick. He was seventy-eight years old and hard of hearing. He seldom left his apartment, but I checked on him once a week. The apartment below mine had been empty up until the previous month. A family of four had recently moved in. The two young girls were four and five and loud. They were one of the reasons I started looking for a house again.

Thankfully, it was a school day, and no one was home yet. I unlocked my door and let Harry in. He quickly ran to his food bowl and sat. With a laugh, I fed him before heading into my extra bedroom which I used as an office.

Pandora immediately joined me. She was a small, black, shorthair domestic cat. She and Harry got along okay as long as Harry did exactly what Pandora wanted. The cat curled up on the couch I have in the room that folds out into a bed when I have guests, and Harry settled on the floor.

The Internet was a wonderful thing. Especially for snooping into a person's life. A quick search showed me that Brandy Perez had both a personal and business online presence. Apparently, Brandy ran a cleaning service called Brandy's Handy Maids. It had a 4.5 rating with thirteen reviews. That was pretty impressive considering the size of Reed Hill. My own store only had twenty-eight reviews, and we had been open for almost seven years.

There was one two-star review on Brandy's page. The woman claimed something had been stolen, but Brandy had replaced it and refunded her the cost of the cleaning so the woman gave her the two stars for effort. I recognized the name on the review and grimaced. Heidi Parker was a habitual complainer and the mayor's wife. I had dealt with her before and could sympathize with Brandy. Nothing else on the business page stood out.

Brandy's personal social media was a different story. She had accounts on all the major channels and posted a lot of pictures. Mostly pictures of her with men drinking and partying. I checked her stats and found she was thirty-nine. Seemed a little old to be on the party circuit.

Brandy had been beautiful. She had shoulder-length brown

hair with highlights. Her face was round with a high brow and full pouty lips. She had a Playboy bunny look. According to the page, she'd lived in Reed Hill all her life. Her relationship status was listed as single, but there were several recent references to a new love. She never stated his name and never posted any pictures of the two of them. However, the pictures of her with other men had stopped. She even made a comment about attending an upcoming private party at a new restaurant in town.

Marcus did not have any social media accounts, but Mike did. He didn't seem very active on the two channels I used; however, he appeared to be more active on other social media sites where I didn't have an account. I was considering creating an account just to contact him when I found Arabella. She was extremely active on her pages, posting pictures of food and her garden. I sent her a message and within a minute had a response. Ten minutes later, I was driving across town.

Arabella Cantono lived in one of the newer subdivisions. Her house was modest compared to some of the others—a one-story home with a brick façade. It looked nice but had no character. I wanted an older home because many of the newer ones looked like all the others.

Arabella was a small, plump woman with dark hair like Marcus. She had a lovely face and the same startling blue eyes as her son. She ushered me into the kitchen and sat a cup of coffee and a plate of cookies in front of me. Both were delicious. She sat and looked me over.

I had only met Arabella at Marcus's restaurant with Marcus and other people around. I found her charming, but direct. This was a woman who pulled no punches.

"So how are you going to save my son?"

I choked on the cookie and had to cough several times before I could answer. Arabella rose, filled a glass with water, and handed it to me. She patiently waited until I stopped coughing before prompting me again.

"Well?"

"Well, what?" I demanded. "What do you mean how am I

going to save your son?"

"Pssh," she replied with a wave of her hand as she sat back down. "You look into things like this."

"Things like what?"

"Murder."

It was true I had helped catch two murderers, but both had been by pure chance. I was nosy and knew a lot of people who talk to me. It allowed me to learn things the authorities didn't. I was also somewhat stubborn.

"Arabella, I'm not…"

"Don't!" she interjected. "Don't tell me you won't help him. I know you care for Marcus. That woman will not bring him down! I won't allow it."

"Okay, okay. Calm down." Arabella looked ready to explode. I took a deep breath. "Did Marcus know Brandy?"

"Yes. They went to high school together. All of them. Damian, Marcus, Lucy, and Brandy. Damian was the oldest. He was a junior when the others started high school, but they all knew each other. My husband died that year. It was hard on the boys. Damian dropped out of school, but Marcus was determined to finish."

This had happened long before I moved to Reed Hill. What Arabella wasn't saying was Damian dropped out of high school to support the family. That meant picking up where his father had left off by selling drugs to the local teens. Marcus had probably stayed in school as the contact. At least, that was how it had worked when I found their stash of heroin all these years later. Damian and Ricky were running the operation, and Mike had been in high school pushing the stuff, but Marcus was long gone.

He had left town with his wife and three-month-old son. Marcus had moved to California, worked full-time while attending college at night, and finally opened his own restaurant. He returned to Reed Hill because Arabella had a health scare. She had been diagnosed with coronary artery disease. It wasn't serious enough to require surgery but serious enough to make Marcus return home to help his mother.

The first thing he did was shut down the family drug-dealing business. He then moved his mother into his home and tried to find legal employment for the family members not in jail. With Damian's recent release, all the family was back in Reed Hill and under Marcus's control. At least as much as anyone could control the Cantonos.

Marcus's background wasn't clean. I was sure he had broken the law more than once to get where he was today, but he seemed to be making an effort to put his family on the right track.

"Do you know if Marcus has had any contact with Brandy recently?" I asked.

Arabella nodded. "That vixen came by the restaurant last month. She told him she was looking for more work. She wanted to clean the place. She has some type of cleaning service."

"I saw that online. It seems to have been well-received."

"Oh, she was a hard worker," Arabella said. "There's no denying that, but she was looking for a free ride. She wanted a man to take care of her. She was trying to get her claws into Marcus again."

"What do you mean again?"

"Back in high school, Marcus and Lucy were a couple, but they had their ups and downs. Their senior year, they had a fight and broke up for a couple of months. Brandy swopped in. She wanted Marcus. She would invite him to picnics by the lake, and well, Marcus was a boy...he took what she offered. It was a sore spot between Lucy and him when they got back together."

It was generous to call the body of water near Reed Hill a lake. Technically, the name was Reed Hill Lake, but it was small. I had been there a couple of times, and it seemed like the ideal place for teenagers to congregate. There was a wooded area near one entrance and a few small docks. You couldn't ski on it, but it was deep enough for fishing.

"Do you think he's seeing Brandy now?"

Arabella twisted her hands in her lap. She looked worried.

"I don't know. I don't think so, but he's been acting mysteriously. He disappears sometimes, won't answer his phone. When I asked him about it, he said he forgot he had it turned off. Once he did answer, and I thought I heard a woman's voice. He said it was the TV."

I needed to talk to Marcus. I needed to find out more about Brandy. And I needed to do both before Griggs tried to stop me.

"Have you heard from Marcus today?"

"Yes. He called before you arrived. He was meeting with his lawyer. I tried to get him to stop by here, but he said as soon as he was finished with the meeting, he was going straight home."

"I need to talk to him. In person. Can you give me his address?"

Arabella raised her eyebrows. "Of course."

After I had written down the address which was just around the block, I asked Arabella what else she could tell me about Brandy. She didn't know much, but she did mention a friend.

"Autumn and Brandy were close in school. I don't know if they were still close, but I saw her picture online when I looked at Brandy's page."

I pulled up Brandy's social media pages on my phone. I had bookmarked them before I left. Arabella pointed out the picture of Autumn. It had been posted about a month earlier. Autumn was a little plump. She had a cute smile and light hair. It was hard to see much more as the picture was taken in poor lighting. It looked like they were at a bar.

"What's Autumn's last name?"

"It was Lloyd back then," Arabella replied. "I don't know if it still is."

I went to Brandy's friends list and found only one Autumn. The last name was Nichols, but it was the same woman. I didn't know how I was going to find her address, but Arabella said she would ask around and get it for me. I left her with the promise I would do what I could for Marcus and drove around the block to see if I was going to be able to keep that promise.

Marcus's house was bigger than his mother's but was built along the same line. It had the same brick façade but was two stories and a different color. He didn't answer when I first rang the bell, but I had a gut feeling he was home. I pressed repeatedly on the doorbell and wasn't surprised when it flew open a few minutes later. His anger turned to resignation when he saw me.

"Go home, Leah," he said.

"Nope," I replied as I stepped past him.

With a sigh, he shut the door behind me but didn't move. He crossed his arms and glared. I glared back until he shook his head and smiled reluctantly.

"I don't need your help, Leah."

"Oh really? So you aren't a suspect in a murder investigation."

"Of course, I'm a suspect," he growled. "They found my tie at the murder scene, but you don't need to be involved."

My heart sank. "It was your tie?"

I had been hoping it wasn't his. He closed his eyes briefly. When they opened, I knew I had lost him. The mask was on.

"Yes. It was my tie. That's all you need to know. Chief Griggs has all the information, and he's very good at his job. He doesn't need your help, and neither do I." He reopened the door, grabbed my arm, and pushed me outside. "Go home, Leah."

The door shut, and I heard the bolt slide into place. I stared at the door a moment before turning away.

"You may not need my help," I muttered under my breath as I walked back to my car, "but you're going to get it anyway."

CHAPTER 6

Back home, I spent a couple of hours searching the web for anything that might indicate Brandy had an enemy or two and trying to ignore the noise from the apartment below. I jotted down a couple more names of her friends including her last boyfriend, Warren Marsh, but didn't find much else of interest. Griggs called about nine and told me nothing new. He didn't mention my relationship with Marcus again. Instead, he refused to talk about the case at all stating Marcus had specifically asked him not to tell me anything. I hung up in a huff. Arabella called after that with the address of Brandy's friend. By then, it was too late to visit. I went to sleep in a bad mood but woke ready to tackle the case.

Autumn Nichols lived on the same street as Brandy. I drove past the house Tracy had wanted to show me. Nothing looked any different. The pickup was gone, but the house looked exactly the same. The only thing missing was the For Sale sign. The owner must have taken it down to discourage gawkers. Brandy's house was closed up as if she had simply gone out for the day. It made me sad to think a woman had been murdered, but nothing really changed.

I arrived at Autumn's a little after nine. Her social media accounts indicated she worked at one of the local fast food restaurants which didn't open until ten. I was hoping to catch her before she left for work. Autumn's house wasn't as well cared for as Brandy's was. It wasn't as bad as some of the other homes in the neighborhood, but the grass hadn't been mowed, and most of it was weeds. There was quite a bit of peeling paint, but there were no abandoned cars or other junk littering the yard. As a matter of fact, there was a fairly nice looking automobile parked in the driveway that looked familiar.

No one answered the door when I first knocked so I tried a second time. I didn't want to be too aggressive as I wanted Autumn's cooperation. Idly, I looked around while I waited. All the houses were quiet. I wondered what the neighborhood was like in the evening. First thing in the morning, it was certainly dead.

The door opened, and I came face-to-face with another Cantono. Damian Cantono didn't have Marcus's good looks, but he was still an attractive man. Like Marcus, he was tall with dark hair, and they had a similar build. Damian's eyes were brown instead of blue. They were also harder and colder than his brother's eyes. I swallowed quickly and gave him a tight smile.

Damian had no reason to like me and every reason to hate me. Although the FBI had been conducting a sting operation to bust up his drug ring, I was the one who had discovered the heroin and figured out how they were importing the stuff into the states. Damian was out of jail because Marcus had posted bond, but he was still facing charges and a trial. And I wouldn't have been at all surprised if he blamed me.

He leaned against the doorjamb and studied me a moment before saying, "What do you want?"

"I'd like to speak with Autumn. This is her house, isn't it?"

I was pleased to note that my voice was steady. It didn't crack—much. I shoved my hands in my pockets to keep them from shaking and tried to look relaxed. I don't think it worked because Damian smirked.

"What'ya want with Autumn?"

"I wanted to ask her about Brandy. I understand they were friends...you all were friends."

"You sticking your nose into places you shouldn't again?"

I shrugged. Damian hadn't attacked me or slammed the

door in my face. He wasn't acting threatening in any way. He seemed to find me amusing. I took what I could get.

"Yeah, I guess I am. He's your brother. Don't you want someone to help him?"

Damian laughed. It was humorless and harsh. "Marcus don't need your help. He's got a fancy lawyer and knows how to work the system. He ain't going to jail."

My eyes narrowed. "Do you think he killed Brandy?"

He mimicked my shrug. "Don't know. Don't care."

Before I could respond, a woman came toward us. I recognized her as Autumn, but she looked different from her photos. Without makeup, Autumn wasn't very attractive. Her face was blotchy. Her hair was sticking out in all directions, and she looked hungover. She was dressed in an oversized t-shirt. Her eyes widened when she saw me.

"Go put some clothes on," Damian barked.

Autumn jumped and scurried away. Damian turned back to me and opened the door wider before saying in a sarcastic tone, "Come on in."

Steeling myself for the unknown, I followed Damian down the short hallway to the living room. The furniture was a little worn but solid. There were several beer cans and a couple of dirty plates on the coffee table. I didn't see any drug paraphernalia, yet there was the lingering smell of marijuana in the air. The room wasn't clean, but I had seen worse. Damian motioned me to have a seat. I chose the one chair in the room, and he settled on the couch.

"So what do you wanna know?"

"Anything you or Autumn can tell me about Brandy and the people around her. Her social media accounts indicated she was seeing someone. Do you know who?"

"No."

"She didn't mention anyone? Talk about a date? Anything like that?"

Damian shrugged again. "I didn't talk to her much. Autumn might know."

"Autumn might know what?"

She walked into the room. She was dressed in shorts and a t-shirt. She had combed her hair and put on a little makeup. It covered the blotchy complexion, but she couldn't do anything about the bloodshot eyes. She joined Damian on the couch and gave me a sour look.

"Do you know who Brandy was seeing?" I said cutting to the chase. I had a feeling neither one of them was going to cooperate.

Autumn glanced at Damian out of the side of her eyes. He didn't respond. She swallowed once and said, "Don't know. She talked big. Always bragging about stuff. She said she was seeing someone who had money."

"She posted that she was going to attend a private party at a new restaurant in town. Do you know anything about that?"

"You think it was my mom's birthday party?" Damian asked with a snort. "Marcus wouldn't have invited her to that."

"Was Marcus seeing Brandy?"

"Don't know. Don't care."

"You don't care about much where Marcus is concerned, do you?"

He glared at me. "Everyone knows my little brother and me aren't close."

"He got you out of jail. You're working at his restaurant."

I don't know why I was egging him on. I didn't like his attitude, but I didn't need to give him any more reasons to hate me.

"Condition of my release was that I had to be gainfully employed," he said with a sneer. "Who else would hire me?"

No one. Which, in my mind, should have made him grateful to Marcus instead of resentful. I turned back to Autumn.

"She didn't give any hint?" Autumn shook her head and picked at a spot on her arm. I pushed a little more. "Do you think she was dating Marcus?"

"Maybe. She talked about meeting the guy at the lake and late at night after business hours. The lake's where she and Marcus hooked up in high school. She said it was like old times."

"They met at the lake?"

"Yeah. She said it was their secret place." Autumn rolled her eyes "Everybody knows she'd just take one of the boats to the other side. Wasn't all that secret. There's a little picnic area over there with a small cabin. That's where she useta meet all the guys."

In for a penny, in for a pound, I turned to Damian. "Where were you the night before last?"

He stared at me a minute and then threw his head back and laughed. At that moment, I could see the resemblance to Marcus. He looked at me and grinned.

"I should've guessed. You ain't gonna pin this on me. I haven't ever killed anybody. I was here all night long. Right, Autumn?" Autumn nodded vigorously. "Besides, I'm not the one in the family with a history of being questioned for murder."

"He was cleared of that," I said defensively.

Damian gave me a sly grin. "Like I said. He knows how to work the system."

He rose suddenly and pulled Autumn up with him. "Time for you to get ready for work."

They both looked at me. With a sigh, I stood and walked to the door. Neither of them said a word as I walked out of the house, but I felt their eyes on me the entire time. I was relieved to reach my car.

My phone had buzzed a couple of times while I had been speaking to Damian and Autumn. I pulled it out and checked my messages. One from Griggs and two from Myra. Myra was my one part-time employee. She was scheduled to work with me that morning. I hadn't worried about getting to the store in time to open it because I knew Myra would. Unfortunately, her messages indicated otherwise. With a soft curse, I started the car and quickly drove across town.

I pulled into the parking space behind my store two minutes before ten. Rushing in, I stowed my purse, grabbed the cash drawer, and hurried up front. Thankfully no one was waiting so I could relax. I unlocked the door and checked the store. Everything was in place.

Traffic in the store was light. Myra's call had been to inform me she would be late. She arrived about ten-thirty full of apologies. Myra was tall and thin. She had lovely auburn hair and a very pretty face. At fifty-six, she didn't need to work. Her retirement income from teaching public school wasn't huge, but it was enough for her to live comfortably as she had inherited a house which sat on a little bit of land. She worked because she enjoyed the contact with people. I was grateful to have her at all. She was reliable and good with our customers. She wouldn't have been late without a good reason.

"Don't worry about it, Myra," I told her. "Is everything okay?"

"No," she said with a snap. "He was at my house."

"He?"

"Leon!"

"Oh, no."

Leon, of pitchfork fame, was a despicable human being. Without his help, I doubt my distant cousin would have gotten as far as he did in his scheme to steal from me. Wade had been the mastermind, and Leon had been a hired hand, but his contributions were what caused me to go along with Wade's demands. Wade had known I would do anything he said in order to protect Myra and Aaron. In the end, Myra had taken care of Leon by hitting him in the back of the head. The police had taken care of Wade by shooting him in the chest before he could shoot me. Wade didn't make it, but Leon only had a concussion.

"I thought he was still in jail," I said, trying to hide my anger. Myra already felt guilty about Leon's behavior. It didn't matter how many times I told her it wasn't her fault. She still blamed herself.

"He's out on bail," Myra replied.

"Who would bail him…Oh…" I stopped.

"She loves him. He has her convinced that it was all a big misunderstanding, and that he's sorry."

Shaking my head, I sat on the stool behind the counter. Myra was referring to her daughter, Jill. Leon had been a terrible husband but apparently a really good father. The dichotomy of that still confused me. How someone could be so loving and supportive to a child but so hateful to that child's mother was hard to understand.

"Are you in danger?" I asked her.

"No," she said with a slight smile. "He's afraid of me now. If I report him, they'll throw him back in jail in no time."

"So what did he want?"

"He claimed he wanted to apologize. Make amends. Same old story. He asked if he could stay with me since he can't leave the county."

"Are you kidding me?" I exclaimed.

"No. He actually asked. He said he wouldn't be in the way, and Jill would pay his expenses until he got a job."

"Unbelievable. What did you say?"

"I didn't say anything. I just walked to the barn and picked up my pitchfork. He took off then." I laughed. I could picture her standing in the doorway with the pitchfork in her hands. "Anyway, I didn't want to leave the house until I knew he was gone. He ran to the road and last I saw him he was walking back toward town."

"The county is big. If he's smart, he'll make his way to McKinney. They have a homeless shelter there."

"Jill won't like that. She'll probably give him enough money to stay at a hotel." Myra grimaced. "I hate that he's taking advantage of her. She and her husband don't have a lot of extra money, but Jill will give him everything she has."

"Myra, it's not your problem. Please don't make it your problem."

"I won't," she said unconvincingly.

Myra was a kind woman. She wouldn't want her child to suffer. I hoped she was strong enough to say no to Jill and to Leon. I also hoped Leon wouldn't show his face anywhere near me. I wasn't sure how I would react, but I knew it wouldn't be good.

"Enough about that dirt bag," she said quickly. "Tell me what you've been doing to clear Marcus."

"What makes you think I've done anything?"

"Because I know you. So give."

With a smile, I told her about my online search for Brandy and my morning with Damian and Autumn. By the time I finished, Myra was nodding.

"Kyra gets in at noon today. After lunch, you can go investigate. It shouldn't be too busy today."

I opened my mouth to tell her I didn't need to investigate, but we both knew I was itching to do just that. Instead, I gave her a smile and agreed. Kyra arrived on time, Myra went to lunch, and then I was free. Free to investigate. Free to snoop. Free to find something, anything that would prove my friend's innocence.

CHAPTER 7

Before leaving the downtown area, I went by Nora's Bakery and picked up two of their lunch specials. Walking back past Scents and Sensibility, I turned onto Main Street and continued until I reached the end of the block. Thompson's Rare Books was a cliché of an old, dark, dusty bookstore. The lighting was dim, and there was a musty smell in the air. Bookshelves lined the walls and aisles. It wasn't very large so the inventory was small, but the books were rare, exquisite, and out of my price range.

The owner, Daniel Thompson, was a grumpy old man who hated parting with his books. He refused to sell to anyone he didn't like and had a reputation of being stingy and mean. He had no employees, never opened on Saturdays, and always closed promptly at six.

I loved the old man. We had an odd relationship. For years, we had an understanding. I could browse his books, even read some while in the store, as long as I didn't talk to him. Of course, I took that as a challenge and somewhere along the way we became friends.

When Wade Collins was in town killing Donnie and attempting to rob me, he murdered a man by the name of Jose Alvera. Jose had been a weird man, but he was loyal to his family. They needed money, and Jose allowed himself to be drawn into illegal activity. His part might not have actually been illegal, but it had cost him his life.

After he died, I had discovered he and Daniel had been friends. As far as I knew, Jose and I were the only two Daniel had. Jose's death hit him hard. Since then, I had made a point of having lunch with the old man every Wednesday. Daniel refused to leave his store so I brought the meal to him.

As I was opening the door to Thompson's, a toddler waddled up to me. He stopped inside the doorway and smiled. I smiled back. His harried mother came running and scooped him up with a quick apology. The little boy waved as they hurried away.

"Shut the dang door, girl!"

Turning back around, I grinned. "Hold your horses, Daniel. I'm coming."

There were two customers in the store which was rare. One of them was Penelope Lansford. Penelope was the owner of The Reed Hill Café, the largest restaurant in the downtown area, and the only one with a formal setting. Before Bella's opened, it was *the* place to have a dinner date. During the lunch hour, they had a home-style menu, but in the evening, it was far more formal.

"Hi, Penelope," I said.

"Leah," she replied with a nod.

Penelope wasn't the friendliest person. I was always amazed at the type of people who go into the customer service business. You would think they would be outgoing and people-oriented, but I've found that often was not the case. Penelope and Daniel were two examples. Unlike Daniel, Penelope was always polite but cold and impersonal. She was precise, detail-oriented, and focused. Her physical appearance reflected that personality. In her late forties, she was neat, sturdy, and strong. She was also the current president of the Downtown Business Association. Most of us didn't like her as a person, but she was great at organizing our fundraising campaigns or special events.

She glanced at the bags in my hand but didn't comment. I tried not to feel guilty about always eating from Nora's instead of the café. They had a to-go menu at lunch, but the bakery was so convenient.

"I understand you found another body," she said sharply, "and that Cantono is involved."

I stiffened. Penelope had never said anything bad about Marcus when I was around, but his restaurant had to be cutting into her business. Maybe I needed to add her to my list of suspects.

"The police are looking at all leads," I replied diplomatically.

She snorted. "They shouldn't need to look any further. That man and his family are a menace. The whole lot of them should be locked up."

"Penelope," I said cuttingly, "Marcus didn't do it. And if the police can't prove it, I will."

With pursed lips, she replaced the book she was holding onto the shelf and walked out. The door shut behind her with a soft, but firm click.

"Wow," said the other customer. "I'd heard Penelope could be a bitch."

I grinned at Alan York. Alan worked part-time at the public library. Like me, he was a regular at Thompson's Rare Books. Unlike me, Alan occasionally purchased something. He was tall and well-built with broad shoulders and dark hair. Alan was fairly quiet, but I found him intelligent and interesting. We shared a love of books. He had a wonderful, soothing voice. Occasionally, I would be at the library when he was reading to the children, and I would stop just to listen to his voice.

"She's usually more subtle."

"I wouldn't want to be on her bad side. Glen has been trying to woo her into helping him get a spot on the square."

"Glen is opening a store?" I asked, surprised.

Glen Davis ran Antonio's with his father, Robert. It was a local Italian restaurant. Nothing like Bella's. It was much more casual. It was the type of place where you relaxed and met friends. You placed your order at the counter, and someone brought it to the table when it was ready. They also did a brisk business in to-go orders. I had picked up a pizza from them last week.

Glen was Alan's husband. Reed Hill didn't have a large gay community, and the town was still conservative enough to make things difficult for a couple like Glen and Alan. In general, they were accepted and well-liked, but there were still a few holdovers. Penelope might be one of them.

"He wants to open another Antonio's on the square," Alan said. His hands tightened briefly on the book he was holding. "He and Robert have been saving up. It's all he ever wanted."

"Is Penelope giving him a hard time?"

"Yes," he snapped. "She's been giving him the runaround. Setting up meetings and then canceling or simply not showing up and saying she forgot."

That didn't sound like Penelope at all. The woman was organized and responsible to a fault. There had to be a reason she was treating Glen in such a manner.

"I'm sorry to hear that. I can try to talk to her if you think it would help."

"Probably not." He huffed and shook his head. "Are you really going to look into the murder?"

"I'm going to ask questions. See if I can learn anything the police can't."

"Isn't that dangerous?" Alan asked.

I laughed. "I'm nosy, and I like to snoop."

"Well, be careful. We would hate to see you hurt again. Candace almost took you out."

I gave him a smile. "You sound like Gabe and Olivia. And Griggs."

"Yeah. It's a terrible thing when your friends want you to be safe," he said, humor lining his voice.

Daniel snorted. Turning to him, I raised my brow in question. He glared at me but greedily eyed the bag in my hand. I placed it on the counter and started removing the items. Daniel scurried around to the front. He walked over to Alan.

"You need to leave," he said.

Alan looked stunned, and I had to hold back a laugh. Daniel pointed toward the door and made a shooing motion.

He pulled the book out of Alan's hand and gestured at the door. "Out. We're closing for lunch."

"Oh…sure…okay."

Alan looked at me. I grinned and raised my hands. Alan chuckled before walking to the door with Daniel on his heels. As soon as the door closed behind him, Daniel turned the lock and flipped the Open sign to Closed.

"Daniel," I said laughing. "That's no way to treat a customer."

"He wasn't going to buy anything anyway," Daniel replied as he walked back over to me. "He'd been browsing for over an hour. What's for lunch?"

I shook my head, and I opened the containers. As Daniel and I ate, I told him about my week. The old man didn't talk much, but he grunted in all the right places.

"I remember her," Daniel said when I finished.

Startled, I asked, "Who? Brandy?"

"Yep. Always after boys, that girl was. What we used to call loose in my time. Don't know what they would call her today."

"Brandy wasn't that old. How did you know her?"

"Didn't say I knew her. Just that I remembered her." He paused, and a sad look crossed his face. "My wife knew her."

"Your wife?" I said softly. Daniel seldom talked about his wife. She died around the time I opened Scents and Sensibility. From everything I had heard, she had been a sweet, caring person. No one had understood why she had married someone like Daniel, but I did. Under that grumpy exterior was a kind and gentle man.

"Yeah," he said. "She used to work—or I guess volunteer—at the library. Kinda like Alan, but she didn't get paid. That Brandy girl would go there a lot. She liked to read. Wanda got to know her pretty well."

"Huh," I said.

Brandy hadn't seemed like the type of person who spent time in the library. All indications were that she had been a party girl. Lots of drinking and barhopping.

"A person can be more than one thing," Daniel said when I

mentioned that.

"I guess you're right. Do you remember anything else about her?"

"Not much more than you already know. She spent a lot of time at the lake, and she dated those Cantono boys."

"Wait. Boys? She dated both Damian and Marcus?"

Daniel shrugged and took another bite. He thought a moment while chewing. "Everyone knew about Marcus. She made sure of that, but Wanda said the older boy picked Brandy up from the library from time to time. 'Course she said lots of guys picked up Brandy from time to time."

"Really? Who else?"

"Aw, Leah. I don't know. It was over twenty years ago. Only reason I remember the Cantono boy was because Wanda was worried about it. We all knew he was trouble."

I set my fork down and leaned back in the chair. "Guess it doesn't matter. As you said, it was twenty years ago. I need to find out who she's been with more recently."

We finished our lunch in silence. Daniel wasn't much of a talker, and my mind was on other things. I tidied up the counter and said goodbye. Daniel just grunted.

Closing the door behind me, a movement caught my eye. I turned around and looked across the street. A man was hurrying down the sidewalk. There were several other people milling around so I couldn't be positive he was the movement I had seen, but it was Ricky Cantono. I stood there wondering why he would be in the downtown area and why I had noticed him. He quickly turned a corner and disappeared from sight.

While I walked back to the store, I mulled over what the old man had said. Three different people had mentioned the lake. Arabella, Autumn, and Daniel. It seemed ridiculous that Brandy would still be meeting men there when she had her own home, but maybe she thought it was romantic. It was worth a visit.

I checked on Myra and Kara and ran by the apartment to let Harry out. I considered taking him with me, but Harry loves water and mud. I didn't want to spend all my time trying to keep him from getting dirty. Hardening my heart when he gave me a forlorn look, I closed the apartment door behind me and returned to the car.

Reed Hill Lake was located about twelve miles north of downtown on the outskirts of the city. I took Oak Street before turning onto Lake Drive which would take me directly to the entrance. Although not a major street, there were several cars on the road. I passed a couple of housing divisions, but development dwindled the closer I got to the lake. The main road continued around the lake and then north into Oklahoma. Before I turned onto the small paved road that would take me to the picnic areas and docks, I glanced in the rearview mirror and saw two cars behind me.

I turned onto the road and idled. Both cars continued north, but as the second one went by, I thought I saw Ricky Cantono again. Was he following me? Ricky and I weren't friends. He didn't like me at all, but I had helped the police find his missing girlfriend. Shrugging it off as a coincidence, I continued down the road. There was a small parking area near the tables. My car was the only one. I parked and got out. I stood still a moment, looking around. There wasn't much to see.

Four picnic tables were on the left. There were two grills behind the tables. Trees surrounded the picnic area although most of the rest of the area was open. The lake itself wasn't big. Maybe a mile long. The area with the tables was the narrowest part. It was probably about two hundred feet to the other side.

There were two small wooden docks. Motorboats were prohibited on the lake. There was nowhere to unload one even if someone was brave enough to try navigating the shallow waters, but there were a couple of rowboats and a kayak tied to the docks. I could see another dock, two picnic tables, and a small building on the other side. Another rowboat was tied to the dock over there.

Autumn had said Brandy's secret place was the cabin. It was worth a look. For a moment, I considered walking around the water to the other side, but the small trail looked like a long hike, and I couldn't tell if the path reached the cabin. Instead, I walked to the dock to study the boats. The first one didn't look safe. It was leaning to one side with some water in the bottom and had only one good oar. The second oar was broken and lying on the dock. However, the other rowboat looked sturdy. There were no leaks, and both oars were in good shape.

As I knelt on the dock to get a closer look, instinct caused me to shift to the right. I hadn't heard or seen him, but the blow came at me from behind. Because I moved, the large object hit the side of my head behind my ear instead of directly on the back of my skull. Unable to keep my balance, I tumbled off the dock into the lake. Dazed and disoriented, I gulped in water. Coughing and spewing, I tried to rise to my knees. Luckily the water wasn't very deep, but it was still up to my chin. Frantic and gasping for air, I tried to get to my feet but slipped on the muddy ground and fell back into the lake, swallowing even more water.

Grabbing the edge of the rowboat, I managed to pull myself up. My head was spinning, and I was coughing up water. I couldn't see much as little black dots obscured my vision, and water was dripping down my face. My hair was plastered across my eyes. I tried to push it back, but my hands were shaking and uncoordinated. Panic was setting in. Heart pounding, I tried to make it to the shore. I stumbled and fell again. Finally, I was able to crawl forward and land at the edge of the lake. Spewing up more water, I was seeing stars and feeling like I was about to black out. I fought it as I knew I wasn't safe.

A shadow fell over me, and a pair of shoes came into view. Sucking in air, I squinted, trying to see who it was. He blocked out the sun, and I couldn't lift my head. As he stepped closer, the sound of a car and loud music filled the air. I heard a curse, and the shoes disappeared. Unable to keep the darkness at bay any longer, I allowed it to take me.

CHAPTER 8

The ceiling tiles were square and pitted. When I opened my eyes, the whole world was blurry, but I could make out the tiles. There was something sticking me in the arm and the sound of a machine beeping nearby. With a soft moan, I closed my eyes tight. I recognized the ceiling. I was in the hospital—again.

"Leah."

A hand touched my arm. The voice was soft with a hint of anger. I reopened my eyes and saw a blob. It took a moment, but it slowly came into focus. Shoulder-length blonde hair framing a pretty face with sky blue eyes and a slightly upturned nose. Eyebrows drawn together, Olivia frowned at me. As I forced a smile, her shoulders relaxed.

"How are you feeling?" she asked.

"Okay," I croaked.

Wincing, I tried to sit up. It didn't work. I fell back onto the pillow with a groan. Olivia raised the bed and held a cup with a straw in front of my mouth. Gratefully, I sipped the cool water. I glanced around and saw that I was in a room. In December, I had been taken to the hospital twice. Once when I had been run off the road by Candace. That time, I spent a few hours in the emergency room. The next time was when I had been strangled by Candace. She had pounded my head into the floor, causing a mild concussion. The doctor had kept me overnight. This felt similar, but my head hurt worse. It looked like I had been admitted again.

"How long..." I asked and leaned my head back. It was throbbing.

"You've been unconscious for over three hours. The doctor said you have another concussion, but he's more worried about how much water you inhaled."

I started to shake my head but stopped when a shot of pain caused me to gasp. Olivia stepped closer. I waved her away and closed my eyes as I breathed slowly. I tried to focus on what Olivia had told me. Something was wrong with what she had said.

"Water," I muttered.

"What?"

"I didn't inhale that much water."

"Are you sure? You were soaking wet, and the kids said you were lying at the edge of the lake with just your head out of the water. The doctor said you might have water in your lungs. He said there's a slight crackling sound in your chest."

Maybe I had inhaled more than I remembered. My chest did hurt, and it was hard to breathe. I swallowed and cleared my throat. My mind was fuzzy, and thoughts were running through my brain, but I couldn't catch them. Everything was just out of reach. I finally gave up and fell asleep.

The next time I woke, the pain wasn't as bad, and it was easier to breathe. It still took me some time, but the room came into focus quicker. Olivia was sitting in the chair by the window reading a book. It looked like she had been there awhile. I coughed a little, and she looked up with a smile.

"Good. You're awake. The doctor stopped by a few minutes ago. He said you had fallen asleep instead of being unconscious which is a good sign."

"So how long was I asleep?" It didn't feel like much time had passed.

"Not long. Less than an hour. You seem much more alert this time."

"Yeah," I said, carefully pulling myself up. "My head's still throbbing, but the searing pain is gone."

"That's good. You have a nasty bump on the back of your head."

Gingerly, I raised my hand and felt my head, flinching when I came into contact with the wound. There was a bandage, and part of my hair was missing. A chunk of hair. I closed my eyes for a moment. In general, I wasn't a vain person. I wasn't ugly, but I had never be considered beautiful. I was okay with that. One of my sisters was gorgeous. I saw how people treated her. Good looks opened some doors, but they came with their own set of problems.

People liked me because of my personality. I made friends easily and had never been worried about my appearance. Although my looks had never been an issue, my one truly attractive physical feature was my hair. It was dark brown, thick, and wavy. By the feel of things, a large section of it had been chopped off.

Olivia gave me a compassionate look. "They had to cut it to stitch up the gash."

My eyes filled with tears. I quickly blinked them away. I was alive. I was safe. That was what mattered most. Olivia patted my arm.

"Did they catch him?" I asked.

"What? Who?" Olivia had a bewildered look on her face.

"The guy who hit me. Did they catch him?"

"Someone hit you?" she shrieked.

"Liv!" I said, rubbing my temple.

"Sorry." She stared at me. "We thought you fell and hit your head on the dock or the boat. Are you saying someone hit you?"

"Yeah. Someone hit me. With an oar. I think."

Olivia muttered a few choice words and pulled out her phone. Twenty minutes later, Griggs arrived with Megan Ross in tow. They both asked how I was but then began peppering me with questions. I had to tell them to slow down. Griggs took over and deliberately asked me each question. I relayed what I remembered which wasn't much. I hadn't seen the man's face. I had a vague impression of him being tall with broad shoulders.

"Shoes," I whispered softly.

"What?" Griggs asked.

"He had dress shoes…" I stopped and closed my eyes. I could hear Megan and Griggs discussing the scene. They were speculating about footprints. I tuned them out and tried to hide my dismay. I remembered the shoes. I remembered Marcus had a pair of shoes just like the ones worn by the man who hit me.

Could he be behind this? Was I wrong about him? I swallowed and tried breathing through my nose. Ricky had been following me, but I knew he hadn't been the one to swing the oar. He wasn't large enough. Had he been working for his uncle? Did he report where I was going? I could feel my pulse start to race, and I had trouble catching my breath. I had to calm down. Griggs was still talking to Megan, but Olivia noticed.

"Leah," she said quietly, touching my arm. "Are you okay?"

The voices stopped, and I could feel all eyes on me. I took another breath and reopened my eyes. I gave her a weak smile.

"My head hurts."

Griggs stepped closer. "We won't stay much longer, but do you remember anything else? The color of the shoes? Tassels or laces on them? Anything like that?"

"Uh. Black, I think. Dark anyway. No tassels or laces. Slip-ons."

It was the truth. I didn't tell them that they looked like Marcus's shoes. I didn't say I had seen shoes like them before. In spite of my doubts, I wasn't ready to throw Marcus under the bus just yet.

"All right," Griggs said. "We'll check for shoe prints. The kids who found you were traipsing all around so there probably aren't any viable ones left, but we'll check."

"What were the kids doing there?" I asked.

"Skipping their last class of the day," Megan said with a snort. "The schools are still shorthanded because of the flu so the high schoolers didn't have any trouble slipping out. They got more than they bargained for though. Not only did they get caught, they thought they had found a dead body."

I laughed softly and closed my eyes again. Griggs and Megan said goodbye to Olivia. I heard the door open and close so I was startled when I felt cool lips on my forehead. My eyes flew open, and I was looking into beautiful green eyes. He gave me a smile.

"I'll stop by later to see how you're doing," he said quietly.

"Okay," I replied. "Uh, wait."

"What?"

"I remember something else. I think Ricky Cantono might've been following me."

I might not be ready to throw Marcus under the bus, but I had no problem fingering Ricky. I was sure he was the man in the car. He might not have been following me, but he was in the area, and Ricky Cantono had threatened me before.

Griggs stilled. "Ricky?"

"Yeah. I thought I saw him on the square when I was leaving Thompson's Books after having lunch with Daniel. And later when I pulled onto the road that takes you to the picnic area, a car drove by, and it looked like Ricky was driving."

"Why would he be following you?"

"I don't know. I can't prove he was. I just thought I should mention it."

"I'll talk to him. Check out his shoes," Griggs said as he quietly walked away.

I spent the rest of the evening dozing, watching a little TV, and receiving visitors. Emma, Myra, and Kara all stopped by to see how I was doing as did several other people who worked downtown. Daniel Thompson even came by briefly. He looked in the door and grunted before turning around. Olivia thought it was odd, but it was his way of checking on me.

Olivia stayed with me the whole time. I tried to get her to leave, but she refused until Griggs returned. It was then I realized they didn't want to leave me alone. I didn't think anyone would come after me in the hospital, but Griggs wasn't taking any chances. He told me he couldn't find Ricky and didn't feel comfortable leaving me alone until he had a chance to talk to him. Griggs sat with me until I fell asleep.

The next morning I felt much better. I still had a slight headache, but most of the pain was gone. Olivia arrived with a change of clothes, and the doctor released me around ten. The concussion was worse than the one I had received in December, and with it being the second in four months, the doctor warned me to be careful. Olivia wanted me to stay with them, but I needed to be in my own space. I wanted to sleep in my own bed with my dog at my feet and my cat by my side.

The drive from the hospital was tense. Olivia was worried, but I had no way to reassure her. Someone didn't want me looking into Brandy's death. I wasn't going to stop so I had no comforting words to offer my friend.

When we arrived at my apartment, Gabe was there with Harry. The Westons had taken him to stay with them overnight. My dog greeted me with delight. He was shaking and ready to jump on me when Gabe grabbed him by the collar to hold him back. I sank to my knees and gave the dog a hug. Glancing around, I didn't see Pandora.

"She isn't happy," Gabe said. "Last I saw her, she was headed into your bedroom, but when I looked in there, I didn't see her."

"She doesn't like being left alone overnight," I replied. "She's probably under the bed. She'll come out when she's ready."

I walked over to the couch. Harry followed and jumped up to sit beside me. Gabe and Olivia stood awkwardly, unsure what to say or do. I smiled and waved them to the chairs.

"It's okay. I'm not going to break."

Olivia huffed and walked to one of the chairs. She perched on the arm and looked at me. "We're worried. You've been run off the road, almost strangled, kidnapped, and almost shot. All in a matter of months."

I winced as her voice rose higher with each word. Olivia was my opposite in so many ways. Petite, blonde, and cute, she had an IQ well above average. She majored in chemistry with a minor in physics and seldom had to crack a book. She did because she loved to study, but she was just naturally smart. What we did have in common was our slightly sarcastic sense of humor, our philosophy toward life, and our devotion to those we love. Olivia was worried about me.

"I know, Liv. I don't mean to keep finding bodies."

"It's not finding the body that's the problem. It's searching for the killer!"

"He's being framed."

Somewhere between the hospital and home, I had lost all my doubts about Marcus. Ricky was still high on my suspect list, but I knew Marcus wouldn't have hurt me. One, he was too smart to do something as obvious as follow me to the lake and bash in my head. It was too risky. The chances of being seen were high. The person who had hit me had been very, very lucky the kids hadn't seen him.

And two, Marcus didn't hurt his friends.

"Don't you think the police know that?" Olivia asked. "Alex, Megan, all the others—they're good cops. Let them do their job."

"I know they're good, but all the evidence points to Marcus. Eventually, they'll have no choice. They'll have to arrest him. Look, Liv, I don't think Griggs believes Marcus is guilty, but he will be pressured to find the killer. He can't ignore the evidence." I paused a moment. "Marcus already has a reputation because of his family. He's changing it. People like his restaurant. They like him, but with his past and his family connections, no one will believe he's innocent. If the police have to arrest him…"

"I still don't understand why it has to be you."

"What would you do if all evidence pointed to me as the murderer? Or Gabe?"

"I would let the police…"

She stopped and glared at me. She couldn't even finish the sentence. Olivia would fight to the end to protect someone she loved. I grinned and waited.

"Fine," she snapped. She looked at me and slowly smiled. "What can we do to help?"

Gabe sighed, walked over to the chair, and sat down beside her. He laid his head back on the cushion and crossed his arms. Olivia rolled her eyes and then looked at me expectantly.

"Right now? Nothing. I just want to curl up on the bed with Harry and Pandora and watch mindless sitcoms all day. Tomorrow we'll try to catch a killer."

CHAPTER 9

The next morning, I felt almost normal. My head still ached, but it had receded to a dull throb. The doctor had told me to expect a lingering headache, perhaps some ringing in my ears, and a list of other potential complications. He also said I would probably experience fatigue and to rest as much as possible. I was able to manage the headache with a couple of over-the-counter pain relievers instead of the prescription he had given me. And thankfully, I wasn't experiencing any other symptoms.

After swallowing the pills, I stared at my reflection. My hair was lopsided, long on the right and short on the left. The blow to my head had been at the base of my skull. The hair on that side was cut to the middle of my ear. The bandage covered another part of my hair that I was afraid I was going to lose when I had to remove it. I wiped away tears and told myself to not be silly. It was just hair. It would grow back. Even so, the first call I made was to my hairstylist. She agreed to work me in at eleven.

Olivia had arranged to work in the store, and with Emma's help, they set the schedule for the next two days. April was one of our slower months, but Friday and Saturday were still our busiest days. Olivia assured me they had it covered. As we were closed on Sunday, I had three full days before I needed to return to work.

After speaking with Olivia, I called Marcus. When he didn't

answer, I sent a text. I had left him a message the night before as well. I was determined to track him down even if he appeared to be ignoring me.

Before leaving for the day, I needed to take care of my pets. I wasn't up for a long walk, but I took Harry outside and circled the parking lot. He seemed content. He had spent the time I was in the hospital with the Weston boys. Harry loved Gabe and Olivia's children, but they were a lot more active than I was. He always came home exhausted.

I took some time to review Brandy's social media pages again. I made note of the men and women who appeared in her feed the most often. I added two more names to the ones I had already marked. I included Heidi Parker, the woman who had given Brandy's business a two-star review. Heidi was a pain, but she was also a gossip. She might know something. Armed with the little information I could gather, I left for my hair appointment.

Jasmin Gale worked in the upscale salon, Le Belle, just off our downtown square. Like Scents and Sensibility, Le Belle wasn't on the main part of the square but one block south on Oak which made it directly south of my store. I had a hair emergency one day about a year after we opened, and Le Belle was the nearest salon. Luckily, Jasmin had been available, and she had performed magic. I had been going to her ever since.

Her eyes widened, and her jaw dropped when I walked in. The shock on her face was real. I felt the tears start to well up again. Jasmin swopped over, gave me a hug, and quickly bundled me into her chair.

"We'll cut it short. I'll keep the volume on top, making the front slightly longer, and we can shave the back. It will allow you to have something around your face while the back grows out. Don't worry, Leah. I'll make you look great."

Jasmin helped me remove the bandage and replace it with a smaller one while she carefully washed my hair. As I relaxed in the chair, I heard a few whispers. By now, most people knew I had fallen into the lake; however, no one seemed to know I had been hit from behind. I wasn't going to advertise that fact.

The fewer people who knew I was a target, the better. It's hard to get people to talk to you when they are afraid to be around you.

"So why were you at the lake?" Jasmin asked.

Everyone in town was aware I had recently been involved with a couple of murder cases, including Jasmin. We'd discussed it the last time I had been in so it didn't surprise her when I told her the reason for my visit to the lake.

"Yeah, Brandy loved to go there."

"You knew her?" I asked.

"Sure. I did her hair. She had gorgeous hair."

"What was she like?"

"Brandy was popular, out-going. Determined might be the best way to describe her. She liked to party. Always going to bars or clubs, but she was smart. She had plans."

"What kind of plans?"

"She wanted to have a family, stability, but she didn't have much. Her dad died from cancer a couple of years ago. Brandy spent a lot of time and money nursing him. She was tired and wanted something, or maybe someone, to fix all her problems. She worked hard but was always looking for the next big thing."

"When did you last see her?"

"Oh, two weeks ago I think. I can check my appointment book if you need to know the exact date."

I should've known Jasmin would have information about Brandy. She knew a lot of people. Hairstylists often had the latest gossip, and Jasmin was no exception.

"No. That's okay. What about relationships? Do you know who she was seeing?"

Jasmin sighed as she turned my head to the side. "That was Brandy's problem. She went through men like most women go through shoes. Always looking for someone new. Someone different."

"She indicated online she was seeing someone."

"She talked about a new guy but never said his name. Just that he was in the restaurant business."

My stomach sank. I sat frozen to the chair. Jasmin didn't notice and continued chatting about her customers. I must have made the appropriate responses because she didn't question me, but my mind was on other matters. This was one more indication Marcus was involved. I really needed to talk to him again. I pulled out my phone and sent another text.

"A quick dry and we'll be done," Jasmin announced.

Five minutes later, I got my first look at the new me. The back of my hair was shaved short while the front fell to my jawline. She didn't quite manage to make me look great, but I didn't look bad. The cut was well-done, and it emphasized my eyes. It just wasn't my style.

"So what do you think?" Jasmin asked.

I gave her a brief smile and sincerely told her, "It'll be great for the summer."

She laughed. "Give it a few months. Then we can start reshaping it to your usual style."

It felt weird, but it did look okay. I felt my spirits rise. It would be cooler for the hot summer months. If I had to have short hair, at least it was the perfect time of the year.

I paid for the cut, made an appointment to return in six weeks, and went to my car. I needed something to eat, but I wasn't ready to face all my friends who would be forced to comment on my hair and ask about the accident. Instead of the usual sandwich at Nora's, I drove out toward the highway and stopped at Bella's.

It was in the middle of the lunch hour, but Bella's didn't draw a huge lunch crowd. It was more a dinner restaurant where you lingered over the meal and sipped wine. There were several available tables so I didn't have to wait. I didn't know the hostess, but I saw Mike Cantono and asked to be seated in his station. Mike was Damian's youngest son. He had threatened me when I was trying to find out who killed Isabel Meeks. The Cantono family hadn't wanted me to discover their drug-smuggling operation. It was the same night I first met Marcus.

After all the arrests had been made, and the bad guys sorted out, Marcus had offered both Mike and Ricky jobs and a way out of the criminal life. At first, it looked like both young men would make the transition, but now it seemed to me that Ricky was probably a lost cause. I didn't know why he had been following me, but I had a feeling it wasn't for anything good. On the other hand, Mike had apologized to me and was working hard. He was attending college and seemed to be taking his new life seriously. He was even friendly to me now.

Mike did a double take when he saw me. He gave me a tentative smile while he filled my water glass. He didn't comment on my hair.

"Hi, Leah."

"Hey, Mike. How's it going?"

"Good. What would you like to drink?"

I ordered iced tea and the lunch fettuccine before asking if Marcus was around.

"No," Mike answered. "He's meeting with the contractor for the restaurant in McKinney."

"Your grandmother said he was meeting with him the other day."

"He's having a lot of problems. This is the third one he hired."

"Really? What happened with the other two?"

"The first guy quit. Said he got a better job. Marcus didn't think it was true, but he didn't want someone who didn't want to be around. The second guy wasn't doing any work. Every time Marcus went by the site, the workers were just sitting around. They didn't have anything to do because the construction manager never ordered any materials. Marcus had to fire him." Mike paused. "And now someone is sabotaging the site."

"What do you mean?"

"Some of the materials have gone missing. One of the forklifts was damaged. Graffiti. Things like that."

"That's crazy."

"Yeah. We had a few problems here too." Someone a few tables over waved at Mike, asking for the check. "Sorry, I gotta go. I'll get your order in."

The lunch was delicious, but my mind was on what Mike had told me. If someone was trying to stop Marcus from opening another restaurant, it might be related to Brandy's murder. But would someone murder a person to stop a restaurant from opening?

Marcus still hadn't responded to my texts or phone call so I got the location of the new restaurant site from Mike. He was somewhat reluctant to tell me, but when I told him I would ask Arabella, he gave in. Marcus was scary, but Arabella wasn't afraid of anyone. Mike knew she would give me the information if he didn't.

The new restaurant was going to be called Bella's II. I had teased Marcus that he wasn't being very original. He had glared at me and told me name recognition was more important. He was probably right.

McKinney was located about a twenty-minute drive from my home. Like Reed Hill, it had a downtown area with a square filled with shops. The rest of McKinney, however, was much bigger than Reed Hill. While we had a little over ten thousand residents, McKinney had closer to two hundred thousand. I was familiar with the area as it had a lot of chain stores and restaurants we didn't. It was also the county seat which meant most of the court cases were tried there, and when I was called for jury duty, that's where I had to go.

Bella's II was going to be located at the edge of town so it didn't take me long to get there. It was on one corner and had a chain-link fence surrounding it. It didn't look like much. The slab had been poured, and a basic frame was up, but that was it. However, there was a lot of activity with dump trucks and construction equipment moving around.

Marcus had selected a good location. There was a shopping center across the street that was still under construction. A few of the stores were already open so there were people milling around and cars in the parking lots. The area would be bustling by the end of the year.

There were cars parked along the street in front of Bella's

with a few pulled up onto the curb. I recognized one of them as belonging to Marcus. I turned onto the road, looking for the opening in the fence. When I found it, I pulled in and stopped the car. Directly in front of me was a small security booth with a man dressed in a guard uniform. He immediately began waving me back.

I ignored him, pulled out my phone, and sent Marcus a text. I told him where I was and that I wasn't leaving until he talked to me.

By now, the guard was walking toward my car. I quickly jumped out and gave him a bright smile. I casually leaned against the car, trying not to fall over. Moving fast hadn't been a good idea. I also tried not to look intimidated. The guard was huge, and he didn't smile back.

"You can't park here," he said flatly.

"I won't be here long. I'm waiting for Marcus." The guard scowled and took another step toward me. I smiled and tried again. "You know, the owner, Marcus Cantono."

"I know who the owner is."

His eyes flicked briefly to the street. I turned my head in time to see a kid wearing a baseball cap and sunglasses ride by on a bicycle. The guard tracked his movement for a moment and then returned his glare to me.

"I sent Marcus a text." I waved my phone. "I'm sure he'll be here any minute now. Matter of fact, there he is."

Marcus was walking down the entrance with a man in a construction hat who was carrying some papers. Apparently, I had interrupted a meeting. Marcus didn't look happy. I could almost see the frustration radiating off him as he stomped toward me. When he got closer, his eyes skimmed my face, and he stopped abruptly, eyes widening.

"What the hell happened to your hai…I mean…uh…you look nice."

For the first time since I had woken up in the hospital, I burst out laughing. Marcus continued toward me with the construction guy following close behind. The guard stepped to the side but didn't leave.

"Marcus," I said with a grin. "You really need to work on your delivery. That was one of the most insincere compliments I've ever heard."

He looked at me sheepishly and opened his mouth to reply. Then all hell broke loose.

CHAPTER 10

The sound of gunfire sliced through the air. The loud popping noises made me shake my head. People screamed. Car alarms blared. The noise was deafening. I quickly dropped down to the ground and scrambled toward the car door. Marcus followed me while the guy in the construction hat jumped behind another car. The guard scuttled back to his security booth. He had his phone to his ear.

Marcus grabbed my shoulders. "Are you all right?"

"Yes." I nodded. Mouth dry, I tried to get my bearings. I tried to turn around but fell on my rear. I sat, unable to move. The gunfire was still going. The air was filled with what sounded like hundreds of balloons exploding one after the other in rapid succession. I looked around, trying to catch my breath. People were scrambling around behind the fence and across the street. I could hear yelling and car doors slamming as people rushed to find cover. Soon the screech of tires sounded as the cars were driving away.

My head was pounding, and I was shaking all over. I believe that was why it took me so long to realize it wasn't gunfire. Marcus had pulled out his phone and was calling 911. I rubbed my temples trying to clear the cobwebs which caused a shooting pain to flash through my head. Squeezing my eyes closed, I waited for the throbbing to pass. I eased up to my knees and peered through the window of my car. The guard had also stopped and was looking around. He looked from building top to building top, and then his gaze moved to the area along the fence line. With a heavy sigh, I stood. Marcus clutched my arm and tried to pull me back down.

"Leah!" he hissed.

The noise was lessening with only an occasional pop or ping. There were no bullets hitting the ground. Just the sound of metal being hit with a small rock or nail. I placed a hand on Marcus's shoulder and squeezed. He looked at me a moment. A voice was shouting through his phone.

"It's not gunfire," I told him. He looked at me in disbelief. "Marcus, I know guns. That's not gunfire."

"You know handguns and rifles. That sounds like an automatic weapon."

Most of my experience was with handguns and rifles. I had participated in numerous shooting competitions while in high school and college. I no longer competed, but I still owned a handgun and had a concealed gun license. With all the recent shootings in schools and churches, I had started wondering if I, or any civilian, should be allowed to carry, but that was an argument for another day. Right then, I knew what we had heard was not gunfire.

"Trust me, Marcus. Look."

I pointed to the guard. He was making his way over to us. He was still talking on the phone, but the expression on his face was one of anger and disgust. The man had a military look about him. I had a feeling he had come to the same conclusion I had. He ended his conversation and stopped in front of Marcus.

"Mr. Cantono, I believe that was firecrackers in one of the trash barrels."

He pointed to the right. As I turned to look, the movement caused my head to swim, and I lost my balance. Marcus caught me before I fell, but I had to lean on him and breathe slowly to avoid throwing up. My vision swam. The concussion was catching up with me.

"Leah!" Marcus yelled.

He scooped me up and gestured toward the car door. The

guard opened it, and Marcus set me gently in the seat. He knelt beside me before reaching for the water bottle I had in the holder. He unscrewed the cap and held it to my mouth. I took it from him and took a sip. My head had stopped spinning, but I was unexpectedly incredibly tired.

Suddenly, we were surrounded by police and emergency vehicles. The sirens made me wince, and I had to close my eyes to avoid the flashing lights. Marcus patted my arm and told me to stay put. I couldn't have moved even if I had wanted to. He wasn't gone long, and he returned with a paramedic in tow.

The man looked me over and stated I had simply overdone it. He made me drink some more water before suggesting I take it easy for the rest of the day. Marcus grumbled a little, but I assured him I was fine.

"Okay," he said doubtfully. "Stay here while I talk to the police then I will drive you home."

When he returned, the nausea was gone, but my head still ached. I moved to the passenger seat and handed him the keys. Marcus didn't say a word. He started the car and drove away. I didn't speak until we were away from the construction site.

"Who wants to stop you from opening the restaurant, Marcus?"

He snorted. "If I knew that, do you really think this would still be going on?"

"I guess not, but it has to be related to Brandy."

His hands tightened on the steering wheel. "I don't think it is."

"Why not?"

"Brandy was personal. This, the vandalism, is business."

"Brandy said she was dating someone who was in the restaurant business."

"Well, it wasn't me," Marcus said sharply.

"I believe you, but if she was, that's one big coincidence."

"What do you mean?"

"Someone is trying to ruin your restaurant business, and the woman who is murdered is dating someone who's in the restaurant business?"

He was quiet for a moment. "I can't believe someone would kill her just to keep me from opening another restaurant."

"He was wearing your shoes."

"What?"

"The man who hit me was wearing your shoes."

Marcus cursed and slammed his hands on the wheel. I closed my eyes and leaned back in the seat as he continued muttering to himself. The car slowed. I opened my eyes to see him pulling to the side of the road. When the car stopped, Marcus turned to me. He looked haunted.

"It wasn't me," he said softly.

"I know," I said, placing a hand on his arm.

He stared at me and shook his head. "I don't understand you, Leah."

"Huh?"

"You are a smart, successful woman. There's no reason for you to believe I'm innocent. There's no reason you should believe me at all."

"Sure there is."

"Oh? What?"

"You're my friend."

He turned away and looked out the window. "You need better friends."

"I have great friends," I said breezily. "You just need to understand me better. I don't give up on my friends."

He didn't reply. We sat in silence for a few minutes. Marcus didn't say anything else as he pulled back onto the road. Head in my hand, I leaned against the window, and I thought about what all had happened. I wanted to believe the sabotage of the restaurant was related to Brandy's murder. One bad guy—not two. But Marcus felt Brandy was personal. If that was the case, we had two people after Marcus.

"How did he get your clothes?"

Marcus glanced at me before returning his eyes to the road. "The night Brandy was killed, I was working at Bella's. One of the bartenders and two of the wait staff had to leave because they were feeling ill. My manager called in another waiter, but they were still short-handed. We had a private party booked for the wine lounge and only one bartender. He was thinking about canceling so I told him I could fill in."

"Seems odd that three people all got sick the same night."

"I know. We've had a few issues at that location too."

"Mike mentioned that. What kind of issues?"

"Some of it is similar. Graffiti on the back door. Cars vandalized. But we also had the dumpster enclosure nailed shut. A couple of the staff have been late or had to miss a shift because they had car trouble or a prank pulled on them."

"What about security cameras?"

"The vandal knows where they are. He has disabled them twice, and the other times, he remains in the blind spots. The few glimpses we've caught showed him dressed all in black. He was always crouching or bent over so we can't even guess at a height."

"Did you contact the police?"

He paused. The Cantono family did not contact the police. Marcus had made an exception a few times, but I had a feeling he would try to handle something like this himself.

"They know," he finally said.

Puzzled by that comment, I simply moved on. "Still doesn't explain how someone got your tie and shoes."

"I got home Monday night a little after eleven. I was tired but restless so I changed clothes and went for a drive. I tossed the suit, shirt, and tie onto a chair in the bedroom and kicked off the shoes. It was a long drive, and it worked. When I returned home, I went straight to bed. The next morning the clothes and shoes were gone."

"You think someone came in while you were out. Did they break in?"

"No."

"So who has a key to your place?"

"No one," he said sharply. Then paused. "Mama does."

Arabella might have gone into Marcus's house and picked up his clothes, but she would never use them to frame her own son. Still, the fact she had a key meant someone else in the Cantono family might have used it.

"It doesn't matter anyway," Marcus continued. "The door wasn't locked."

"What?"

"When I went for the drive, I didn't lock my front door."

We lived in a close-knit community, but Reed Hill wasn't so small that people didn't lock their doors. We had crime. Things like petty theft, drugs, and domestic abuse. People enjoyed living in the area, but crime was still a factor. Marcus not locking his door didn't feel right.

"Why on earth did you leave…" I stopped as the lightbulb went off. "You were expecting someone."

He didn't look at me. He ran a hand through his hair, his profile bathed in sunlight. It hurt to look at him, but I was struck again at how handsome he was. Even tired and stressed, he was gorgeous.

"Not expecting exactly. More like hoping."

"She didn't show?" I asked softly.

"No."

"Are you sure?" He shot me a startled look. I shrugged and continued. "Could she have come and gone while you were out? Could she have taken the clothes?"

"NO! She had nothing to do with this, Leah."

"Marcus, you have to consider it. How well do you know her?"

"She isn't involved," he growled.

"Who is it?"

"None of your business. I told you she didn't have anything to do with this."

"Do the police know about her? Do they know you left your door unlocked so she could get in?"

He squirmed in his seat but didn't reply. We were nearing my apartment. Marcus turned onto Ash Street. This unknown woman could have taken his clothes and given them to the killer. If that was the case, Marcus was in big trouble. He obviously cared about her, but he seemed convinced of her innocence.

He pulled to a stop in a parking spot in front of my building. My head hurt, and I was exhausted, but I couldn't get his mystery woman out of my mind. There was something niggling just out of reach. Marcus opened his door and came around to help me out. I don't know what triggered it, but suddenly I knew.

He opened my door, and I looked at him with wide eyes. He closed his briefly and sighed. "Leah…"

"You're dating a cop?" I said incredulously.

"Come on," he said, reaching down to take my arm and help me up from the seat.

He led me to the sidewalk and up the stairs to my apartment. He had to steady me once or twice. I was still a little dizzy so it was nice to have someone at my back. Marcus followed me inside and shut the door behind him.

"Where are your pain pills?" he asked.

"In the bathroom," I replied with a wave toward the hall.

"Why don't you go take one?"

"I will," I said and waited. When he didn't move, I asked, "Aren't you leaving?"

"I'll stay until you're asleep. I wouldn't put it past you to try to go out and start interrogating every female cop in town."

I huffed. "I wouldn't do that. I know I need to rest. Besides, I don't need to interrogate every one of them. I already know who it is. Megan and Marcus. The cop and the criminal."

He glared at me. I walked away. In the bathroom, I downed one of the pain pills and changed into shorts and a t-shirt. I wasn't about to change into my nightgown. It was only three in the afternoon.

When I opened the door, Marcus was leaning against the wall waiting for me. He reached out and took my arm to guide me to the bedroom. I started to shake it off but decided it wasn't worth the effort.

"I can make it to the bed by myself," I muttered.

"I know. Let me help you this time, Leah."

Surprised, I glanced at him. I finally saw the worry on his face. I nodded and let him lead me to the bed. He pulled back the covers, and I crawled in.

"Sorry about the criminal remark," I said sleepily. "That was mean. You aren't a criminal."

He laughed humorlessly. "Sometimes you are so naïve."

"Hey!" I said, knowing I should be offended by that remark, but the pain pill was starting to work, and I was feeling a little loopy.

Marcus leaned down and kissed me on the forehead. It wasn't the same as Griggs, but it was still nice. He smiled at me. "Go to sleep, Leah. You can go back to trying to save me tomorrow."

"Okay," I slurred. "I will, you know."

"What?"

"Save you. No one messes with my friends."

As I was falling into a deep sleep, I heard him softly say, "If anyone can, it would be you."

CHAPTER 11

When I woke a few hours later, I was much more alert. The pain was mostly gone, and I was no longer tired. I just hoped I would be able to sleep that night. After splashing my face with water, I wandered into the kitchen to find something to eat and stopped in my tracks. Griggs was sitting at my kitchen table. He had a laptop in front of him and a few papers nearby. Harry was lying on the floor at his feet, and Pandora was sitting on the windowsill behind him, observing his every move.

Harry saw me first. He jumped up and ran over to me demanding attention. I patted him and made cooing noises while he shook with delight. When I looked up, Griggs was watching me. I gave him a tentative smile.

"How are you feeling?" he asked.

"A lot better," I replied. "What are you doing here?"

"Cantono called. He said you almost passed out at the construction site."

There was censure in his voice which I ignored. I took a couple of steps into the room and waved at the table.

"What's all this?"

"Something to do while waiting for you to wake up." He closed the laptop and laid the papers on top. "Are you hungry? Olivia brought by some meatloaf."

My stomach rumbled at the thought of food. I loved Olivia's meatloaf. I looked at Griggs hopefully.

"And mashed potatoes?"

He laughed and nodded. "And mashed potatoes. Sit. I'll warm it up."

I could have done it myself, but it was nice being waited on. I pulled out the chair next to the laptop and glanced at it. The papers were all facedown. I frowned but stopped myself from turning them over.

A few minutes later, Griggs set a warm plate with a large slice of meatloaf and a scoop of potatoes in front of me. It was quickly followed by a bowl with a green salad and a glass of water. Griggs sat down opposite me, and we both dug in.

Once I had satisfied my hunger, I sat back in the chair and looked at Griggs only to find he was watching me. He looked tired, but he smiled. I smiled back. I realized this was the first time we had eaten alone. By that, I mean not in a restaurant, but just the two of us with no one else around.

"I like your hair," he said softly.

Cocking my head, I studied him. His face was sincere and earnest, but I saw humor lingering in his eyes. With a shrug, I snorted. "No, you don't."

He chuckled. "Well, it's not your style, but it's cute."

Since I didn't know how to respond, I let it go. He seemed relaxed and at home sitting in my kitchen. It gave me a nice feeling so I searched for a safe topic.

"Olivia didn't want to stay?"

"She offered," he said, "but I'm not on duty so I told her I would. I think one of the boys had something tonight anyway."

"Ah, crap. Aaron's little league game."

The Weston boys were involved in a lot of activities. I didn't attend every event, but I tried to go to as many as possible. I had told Aaron I would be at his game.

"I'm sure he knows why you aren't there," Griggs said, rising to pick up the dishes. He carried them to the sink and started rinsing them. "So tell me your take on this afternoon."

"What?"

"Cantono told me about the firecrackers at Bella's II. What did you see?"

I stared at him in shock. He was usually trying to get me to stay out of things. He shook his head and gave me a grin.

"I'm not stupid, Leah. I know enough to pick your brain when I can. You notice more than most people."

The words warmed me. I loved mysteries. Although I did not actively look for dead bodies, I had found more than my fair share. I got sucked into finding the killer because I was curious and needed to know how the story ended. I had always assumed Griggs thought I was sticking my nose into things I shouldn't.

"Thanks," I said and thought a moment. "It was probably the guy on the bicycle."

"What guy on the bicycle?"

"Before the fireworks went off, a guy rode by the site on a bike. He was wearing a baseball cap and sunglasses so I didn't get a good look at his face, but he seemed young. A teenager maybe."

"Did you see him do anything?"

"No, but everything happened a few minutes later."

Griggs finished the dishes and returned to the table. "No proof if you didn't see anything, but I'm sure the McKinney police will ask around. Maybe someone else saw something."

I nodded and ran my finger up and down my glass. Griggs seemed open to talking about his work.

"Someone is framing Marcus," I said tentatively.

He sighed. "I know that, Leah."

"You do?"

"It's fairly obvious. Even the dumbest criminal isn't going to leave his own tie behind. And Marcus Cantono is not dumb." He stopped for a moment. "The problem is the Cantono family's reputation."

"You're getting pressure?"

"The mayor and a couple of councilmen want me to arrest him. Penelope Lansford told me I was biased because you're friends with Cantono, and Glen Davis said I needed to get my department in order. I keep telling everyone we don't have enough proof but…"

"You may not have any choice."

"DNA testing takes a lot of time, but he admitted it was his tie. I could make a case right now. He had a previous relationship with the victim, he was recently seen in her company—more than once, and she had indicated she was in a relationship with him. Or at least someone like him. For some juries, that might be enough."

"And there's his shoes."

"What? What shoes?"

Oops. I had forgotten I hadn't told Griggs that the man who hit me had been wearing Marcus's shoes. I gave him a weak smile.

"Are you kidding me?" he said angrily. "The man at the lake had his shoes? Why the hell didn't you tell me?"

"I did tell you about the shoes. I just didn't mention they looked like the shoes Marcus had. It's not like…" I trailed off as I saw the look on his face. "Marcus didn't do it."

"You keep saying that like your opinion is the only one that matters. The evidence is stacking up against him more each day." He paused. "This is what I meant the other day. Your attachment to him is more than that of a friend."

My eyes widened. "It isn't. I just want to help him. I would do the same for you or Gabe or, I don't know, anyone. Remember how I wanted to help Trent?"

Trent Kearney had been suspected of murdering Isabel. The evidence had been circumstantial, but he'd been arrested because he had been involved with the drug-smuggling. Griggs hadn't been happy when I was determined to free him.

Griggs took a breath. "Cantono is far more dangerous than Trent Kearney."

"You said you knew he was being framed."

"Yes, but I'm a cop. You're not. You're supposed to tell me everything so I can sort out all the facts."

"I've told you most things. I knew it would make him look guilty. If you didn't know, you wouldn't have to act."

He shook his head. "Are you ever going to trust me as much as you trust him?"

The words were a blow. Mostly because they were true. Oh, I trusted Griggs for most things. Trusted him to be a good person, a good man. Trusted him to treat people with respect, but I hadn't trusted him to clear Marcus. I hadn't given him the information he needed to make an informed decision.

Tears swam in my eyes. I tried to blink them back. I wasn't normally a weepy person, but between the concussion and the painkillers, I was a wreck. Griggs's face went from hard to panicked in a flash. He reached for my hand.

"Don't. I'm sorry."

"No," I said. "You don't. Don't be nice to me. You're right. I'm the one who should be sorry. And I am."

Wiping the tears from my face, I took a deep breath and told him everything. He already knew most of it, but I told him what Marcus had said about his clothes. I told him what Arabella and Autumn had told me about Brandy, and what Mike had said about the damage to the restaurants. I even told him what Daniel had said.

"I didn't think about talking to the older generation," Griggs said. "We've spoken to Brandy's friends and employees, but we haven't looked that far in the past."

"I really didn't think about it. I was just talking to Daniel."

"Who else is on your list?"

"What?" I asked innocently.

Griggs rolled his eyes. "Who else are you planning to speak with?"

I shrugged. "I found a few names on her social media pages, and I thought I would talk to Heidi Parker."

"Why?" Griggs asked.

He knew Heidi. Being the mayor's wife, he had a lot of interaction with her. She complained about everything. She had complained to me about one of my products, and she had filed more than one complaint to the police department which was why I wasn't surprised she had shown up on Brandy's page as the one person not satisfied with her cleaning service. Her complaints were never life-threatening, but Griggs had to have someone check each of her grievances which took up manpower he didn't have to spare.

"She gave Brandy's cleaning service a two-star review. It had been one-star, but she changed it after Brandy replaced the item Heidi claimed was stolen. I don't like her very much, but she doesn't lie."

Griggs rubbed a hand across his face. "No, but she reports the most ridiculous things. Once she said she smelled urine in her flower bed so she wanted us to set up a sting operation to catch whoever was peeing in her yard."

"Oh my God," I said with a giggle. "Did you?"

"Cisneros needed some overtime work so I had him sit outside her house a couple of nights."

"And..."

"It was a stray cat."

"I bet that didn't go over well."

"No. Heidi didn't believe us until Cisneros showed her the video he took with his phone. The damn cat walked by three times each night and lifted his leg right in front of her petunias."

Laughing, I shook my head. "Well, like I said, she doesn't lie. She returned two of my products because there was a chip on the plastic jar. One of the shipments hadn't been packed properly so they had jostled around a little. A few of the jars got chips. No leaks. Nothing was wrong with the cream—just the jar. She made a big deal about it, but the jars were chipped."

"See. Ridiculous."

"True, but if one of Brandy's employees did steal something, Brandy might have had to fire them." I paused. "The tone of Heidi's review was malicious. She was extremely upset. She also talks to a lot of people. If she talked to the right person about the theft, they may have said something to her about their dissatisfaction with Brandy."

"That's a stretch," Griggs said.

"I know. It's probably a waste of time."

"Probably, but if you do it, then I don't have to waste resources on it."

"You would have sent someone to talk to her?" I asked, surprised.

"Maybe. Eventually. It would depend on what else we discover. Ross has someone looking at Brandy's social media. She's interviewing all the employees and combing through Brandy's records. Heidi's complaint will be low on the priority list, but if the murder isn't solved, we'll get to it sooner or later."

"I'll let you know what I find out."

I rubbed my hands on my legs, fighting with myself for another moment. There was one more thing I needed to tell him, but I hesitated. Marcus and Megan had kept their relationship hidden for a reason. Did I have the right to expose it? I thought again about trust. Griggs deserved mine.

"So there's one more thing," I said slowly.

"And what is that?"

"Are you aware that Megan is dating Marcus?"

His eyes went flat, and his jaw tensed. I could see the anger on his face. "Are you telling me the lead investigator in this case is dating the prime suspect?"

"Umm, yes. I think."

"You think?"

"When I asked, Marcus said the police knew about the vandalism at his restaurant and his door being unlocked, but he never said he actually reported anything. And Megan told me she had seen Marcus at Bella's the night Brandy had been killed. She recognized his tie. Arabella told me she thought Marcus was seeing someone, and when I questioned Marcus about leaving the door unlocked, he admitted he was expecting someone. I kind of put it all together and came up with Megan. He didn't deny it, but he didn't confirm it either."

"Damn it," Griggs said sharply as he rose from the table. He grabbed the laptop and papers and shoved them into a bag that had been sitting on the floor. His movements were jerky and sharp. The bag slammed onto the table, causing me to jump.

"I guess you're leaving?"

He glared at me then ran his hand across his face. He took a deep breath and waved his hand in an apologetic move. "I have to go ask my top officer if she's dating a suspect. She can't lead this investigation if she's personally involved. The case is already jeopardized by her involvement. What the hell was she thinking?"

Megan was thinking this was a big case. The first one she was in charge of on her own. She'd been the lead on the last murder, but Griggs had followed her every move. Now, she wanted to do a good job, make an impression. And she probably wanted to protect Marcus.

"Are you going to be all right here alone?" Griggs asked me.

"Yes. I feel pretty good."

"Are you sure? I can call Olivia and Gabe."

"No. I'm fine."

"Take it easy. I'll try to call later to check on you, but I don't know if I'll have time."

"I understand. I'm not going anywhere tonight."

Although I did feel much better, the afternoon had gotten to me. I already knew I wouldn't have any trouble sleeping. I followed Griggs to the door. He gave me a quick kiss and left. I thought about calling Marcus to tell him but knew he couldn't do anything to help Megan. He would try to defend her which would simply make things worse. Dejected, I settled on the couch to spend a quiet evening at home. What a mess.

CHAPTER 12

On Saturday, I slept in a little. I didn't have to work, and I enjoyed being lazy for once. I took a leisurely shower and tried to figure out what to do with my new hairstyle. The bandage was no longer needed, but because the cut was red and the stitches unsightly, I put a smaller one on to cover the abrasion. Luckily, my hair fell into to place with just a brush. I still wasn't planning on keeping the style, but it was beginning to grow on me.

Harry and I went for our usual walk in Reed Hill City Park. I took it slow, but it felt good to be outside. My apartment complex has a number of individual buildings with four apartments in each. Mine is toward the front. At the back of the complex, the nicer and more expensive units face the park. I loved our city park. It had walking trails and a bike path. There were lots of trees and grassy areas, and there was a small creek running through it.

In February, I had found the body of my distant cousin lying facedown in the creek. Actually, Harry had found him. I hadn't known Donnie, and he had been a jewel thief and career criminal, but he hadn't deserved to die. As another cousin had been the one to murder him, it had put me off looking for our relatives.

As we neared the entrance, I glanced over at the houses lining one side of the park. On the corner closest to my apartment complex, there was one house with an exceptionally large lot. Because of that, the house next to it was sitting on a smaller piece of land. It was the small Cape Cod style house that had gotten away.

There was a moving truck in the driveway. It and the house appeared to be locked up tight. There was no sign of activity. I desperately wanted a glimpse of the person who had stolen my house, but the new owners had either already unloaded or were waiting for help.

Harry tugged on the leash, and we made our way into the park. The walking path was great. It was wide enough that joggers could easily get around the walkers. Harry and I strolled along, stopping occasionally for him to investigate. I was lost in thought and not paying attention to my surroundings so I didn't see him until he called my name.

"Hi, Leah."

Sean Walters was a struggling artist. Well, his art was struggling, and he played the part by wearing shabby clothes, keeping odd hours, and drinking a little too much. However, he lived in one of the nicer apartments with his father. Sean jogged daily, and I used to see him quite often, but he had been involved with the scheme my cousin had cooked up to rob me. Sean hadn't known all the details, and I didn't blame him for anything, but I hadn't seen him since the night he had told me about his part in the scheme.

"Hi, Sean," I said, giving him a bright smile. I knew he had been avoiding me as my routine was pretty regular. I was in the park later than normal so I probably surprised him.

Sean was a large man, over six feet tall but young and sweet. He was incredibly shy and not very self-confident. It had taken me months to get him to say more than a few words. Things had been easier after I expressed an interest in art.

He shuffled his feet. "Uh, hi, um, how are you?"

"Good. You?"

"Fine,' he mumbled. He took a deep breath. "I never got to say, you know, sorry for everything."

"It wasn't your fault, Sean. Ricky hired you to make the rose."

Ricky Cantono had been involved in the scheme to rob me. He had forced Sean to carve a wooden rose that looked like the one I had inherited from my grandmother. Sean was addicted to Vicodin and found an easy way to get it. Ricky supplied the drug in exchange for Sean's talent. Ricky was being blackmailed too, but that didn't excuse his behavior. The whole situation was one large mess orchestrated by Wade Collins.

Sean rubbed the back of his neck and refused to meet my eyes. "Yeah, but I knew something was wrong."

There wasn't anything I could say to that so we stood there awkwardly. Harry broke the tension by moving closer to Sean, wagging his tail. Sean grinned a little and reached down to pet the dog.

Still not looking at me he said, "Leon Hollins is out of jail."

"How did you know about that?" I hadn't known Sean knew Leon.

"You already knew?" His shoulders relaxed. "Good. That's good."

"What do you know, Sean? What are you trying to tell me?"

"Nothing really. I heard from a friend that he was out and asking around about a place to stay. He's bad news, Leah. Everyone knows what he did. I guess I wanted to warn you. You know, in case, he tries something."

"Myra said he told her he was trying to make amends."

Sean shrugged. "He's been asking around about a way to make some fast money. Offered his services to anyone who'll pay."

A shiver went down my spine. "Services?"

"Selling or, you know, collecting."

Ricky had been Sean's supplier until the drug bust. Sean had told me he had purchased from the Cantonos until the arrests in December when he had to find a new dealer; however, Ricky had found a way to get the Vicodin to him in February. After everything that had happened, I had assumed he had stopped using. It was a stupid assumption.

"Who told you that?"

"Just rumors, Leah."
"Sean…"
"Gotta go."

He suddenly took off. I started to follow, but Sean jogged regularly. There was no way I could catch him. I wasn't sure what he told me meant anything for Myra or me, but if there was a new drug dealer in town, Griggs needed to know.

I had to leave him a message, and Harry and I finished our walk with no further interruptions. On the way back to my apartment, I checked out the house again, but there was still no sign of anyone.

Before I headed out for the day, I spent some time with Pandora and making a list. There were several people I wanted to speak with regarding Brandy. I also needed to pick up the gift I had ordered for Arabella assuming the birthday dinner was still on.

Checking my purse, I pulled out my handgun. I did a quick cleaning and verified that everything was in working order. I had been to the range the week before, and the gun performed fine. My shooting preference was a rifle, but I was proficient in handguns. Griggs had once challenged me to a shooting competition. It had been close, but I had beaten the chief of police. It had been a heady moment. I didn't plan to use the gun but wanted it with me just in case.

I took Harry with me this time. I didn't want a repeat of what happened to me at the lake. The gun wouldn't do me any good if someone came at me from behind. Harry wasn't trained to be a guard dog, but he had good instincts and was very protective. He was incredibly friendly, but most people would hesitate to approach me if he was around.

Our first stop was Harbor Trailer Park. I wanted to talk to Ricky Cantono. I believed he had been following me the day I went to the lake. What I didn't know was why. Ricky probably wasn't involved in Brandy's murder, but something was going on with him. If there was a new drug dealer in town, he would know. Last I heard, he was living with his girlfriend, Vanessa, in her trailer.

Harbor Trailer Park wasn't the most cheerful place to live. Most of the trailers were in disrepair. Many were rusted and had peeling paint. The park itself wasn't large. It had two lanes with trailers on either side, and many of the slots were empty. Vanessa's trailer was small but one of the few in good shape. The yard around it was neat, and the trailer had no peeling paint or obvious flaws.

Ricky had known my cousin, Donnie, who had been murdered. Donnie stayed with Ricky at the Cantono house in Mayville when he was in town trying to steal my great-grandmother's wooden rose. After Donnie was murdered, Ricky had tried to remove himself from the scheme, but my other cousin, along with Leon, needed the local contact. They had kidnapped Vanessa and blackmailed Ricky into helping them. He, in turn, had forced Sean to help him.

At first, I had felt sorry for Ricky. He truly cared for Vanessa, but looking back, I had a feeling it wouldn't have taken much for him to join the others. Vanessa had simply been an excuse. After everything calmed down, Vanessa had been found locked in a bathroom in one of the rooms at the Main Street Inn where Leon had been staying. She had been scared but unhurt. At the time, it had seemed lucky. Now, I wasn't so sure it hadn't been planned.

Although Vanessa had been involved because of her kidnapping, I hadn't met her. All I knew about her was what I had learned from one of her neighbors who had said that Vanessa was a good person. She didn't have the best childhood but was trying to improve her situation. I didn't understand what Vanessa saw in Ricky. She hadn't sounded like the type of person to get involved with him, but Mike had told me in February they had been planning to marry.

I stopped the car, and Harry and I got out. There were no vehicles parked in front of Vanessa's trailer, and I didn't see any sign of the car Ricky had been driving when he was following me. I'm not sure I would've recognized it, but there were no cars that even came close. The trailer appeared to be locked up tight. I knocked on the door anyway, but no one answered.

Turning around, I walked over to the next trailer. The woman who opened the door was the same one I had spoken with the night Griggs and I had tried to find Vanessa. She looked to be in her fifties, but I thought she might be younger. Hard times had taken a toll on her. Her face was thin and haggard, and her hair was starting to gray. Like before, she had a cigarette in her hand.

"Hi, Dee," I said brightly. "Remember me?"

"You're that not cop," she said in her harsh voice.

When I had spoken to her before, she had asked me if I was the police. She didn't like cops. I had answered her honestly, but Griggs had been there. Dee had been worried enough about Vanessa that she had ignored him and answered my questions. She was a hard woman who had been beaten down one time too many, but she cared for Vanessa.

"What happened to your hair?" she asked me before I could speak.

Unconsciously, I raised my hand to my hair. "I got hit in the head. They had to cut my hair to sew up the wound."

I turned my head slightly, showing her the back. She actually leaned forward to look at it. She couldn't see anything. It was covered with a bandage.

"Huh," she said. "Who hit you?"

"I don't know. Probably someone trying to keep me from asking questions."

Dee took a drag from her cigarette, the smoke curling in the air. "So you're sticking your nose in other people's business again."

"That's right." My reputation around town was getting worse. "And I'm, once again, looking for Vanessa."

"What'da want with her?"

I paused. "I guess I'm looking for Ricky. I heard he was living with Vanessa."

"Not no more. She kicked him out a week ago."

"Really? I thought they were getting married."

"Nah. Vanessa changed her mind about that. Told him she

didn't want anything to do with dealing drugs."

"Ricky's dealing drugs?"

"He's a Cantono, ain't he?"

"The Cantono drug-dealing operation has been shut down."

Dee snorted in disbelief.

"You think he's selling again?"

"Saw a couple of deals go down. He had some guy come by a couple of times. Think he was the supplier cause not long after that he had a parade of people through here. Vanessa wasn't home so I told her about it. She confronted Ricky. He said he and his dad needed the money. That's when she kicked him out."

So Damian had started up the old family business. I wondered if Marcus or Arabella knew. It didn't answer my question about why Ricky was following me unless he and Damian had something to do with Brandy's murder after all.

"Do you think Vanessa would know where Ricky is staying now?"

Dee took another long drag off her cigarette, then shrugged. "Maybe, but she left. Ricky kept coming around trying to get her back. Couple of days ago, she got a job in Dallas. She locked up and left. Said she'd be back to get her trailer as soon as she found a place for it."

I glanced around looking for a clue I knew I wouldn't find. Ricky wasn't there. I thought the house in Mayville had been sold, and he hadn't been at Autumn's with his father. Or, at least, I hadn't seen him. I thanked Dee for her help and left.

As I backed the car out, I thought about where I could get more information about Ricky's whereabouts. Mike might know where his brother was staying, but I doubted he would tell me. I knew Marcus wouldn't tell me so that left Arabella. Silently, I added her to my growing list of people I needed to see.

CHAPTER 13

There were four prominent families in Reed Hill. My friends, the Westons, were one of them. Gabe's family had lived in town for over a hundred years. His great-grandfather started the manufacturing business Gabe now runs. By the time Gabe's father had taken over, the plant was the largest employer in town, and it still was.

Gabe and Olivia lived well as did his parents and sister. The manufacturing plant weathered the green movement, changing with the times, and provided a decent living for many of our residents. The Weston family was well-known and well-liked. Gabe was on the city council, and he and Olivia were involved with many community events.

The second prominent family was the Thorpe family. Anthony Thorpe had been one of Candace's victims when she went on her killing spree. I hadn't known him well, but we had started to become friends just before he was killed. His death had been hard on me.

The Thorpe family owned Patina, the store next to mine. They also owned a car dealership and the local movie theater. Next to Weston Manufacturing, the Thorpe family was the largest employer in town. The antique store had closed for a while after the two murders and arrest of one of its employees, but they had recently reopened. Tony's daughter had decided it was worth saving and was currently managing the place.

The third family was Mitchell and Fiona Reed. Mitchell's

ancestors had founded Reed Hill. The couple had no children and were in their eighties. I would occasionally see them around town, but they spent most of their time at home. Their money came from the still pumping oil wells in west Texas.

The Parkers were the fourth family. As mayor, Ben Parker was well-known but not well-liked. He was a womanizer and a world-class jerk. The problem was he was a really good mayor. He had a lot of contacts and had brought a lot of new business into our town. He worked hard and had improved the roads and city parks. I had little doubt he would be re-elected.

No one knew where the Parkers got their money. They moved into town one day about twenty years ago and bought a house. I heard Ben handled some investments and worked out of his home, but that had been before the housing crisis. Now, other than his job as mayor, Ben didn't work. The salary for our mayor wasn't enough to provide the lifestyle the Parkers lived. I would have thought he was making shady deals and skimming the city coffers if he hadn't been living the same way years before he ran for mayor. Of course, the fact that our city coffers weren't very deep helped.

The Parkers lived in a huge house on the north side of town. The neighborhood was as different as possible from the Harbor Trailer Park. Heidi's house was a Craftsman style home with an arched doorway. It was painted a soft gray with white trim and had intricate woodworking around the windows. It was beautiful.

The door was answered by a middle-aged woman dressed in a housekeeper's uniform. I had taken Harry back to my apartment before driving to the Parkers. I knew Heidi wouldn't have let me into her house with a dog in tow.

The housekeeper gave me a polite smile and showed me into the living room after I introduced myself and asked to speak with Heidi. I settled on the small formal couch to wait. I didn't have to wait long. Heidi was a pain in the rear, but she loved to gossip. She wouldn't be able to resist learning what I was doing.

She swept into the room like a soap opera diva, calling me

darling and kissing me on the cheek. I responded in kind. Heidi needed the ego boost, and it didn't cost me anything. She offered refreshments, and we chatted lightly while waiting for the housekeeper to bring tea.

Heidi was an attractive woman. She was probably close to fifty. I thought she was too thin, but she looked good. She dressed in bright colors, and her hair and makeup were always perfect. I had never seen her without at least four pieces of jewelry. All of it large and ostentatious.

"Heidi, I understand you had an issue with Brandy's Cleaning Service."

"Yes, well, I don't like to tell tales…" she said softly.

She loved to tell tales. She just wanted me to pull it from her. I gave her a smile and nodded knowingly.

"Of course not. Brandy's death was unfortunate." I paused for effect. "You know I'm friends with Marcus Cantono. He's been trying so hard to be a good citizen and contribute to society. I'd hate to see him framed for something he didn't do."

Heidi didn't care about Marcus. She gave me a falsely sympathetic smile. "Oh Leah, dear, I doubt he was framed. The Cantonos are not exactly our type of people."

"He didn't do it," I said.

"You would like to think so, but you can't be sure."

"Oh, but I am sure." I leaned forward and whispered, "I have insider knowledge."

Heidi's eyes widened. I could see her running it through her mind. I was dating the police chief. He had proof that wasn't common knowledge. He had passed that information to me. Here was some gossip she could have no one else knew.

I sat back in my seat and waited. I hadn't told her anything confidential. I hadn't said where I had gotten my insider knowledge. It wasn't my fault she assumed it was from Griggs and not my own belief in Marcus.

"In that case, I guess I can tell you." I nodded but didn't speak so she continued. "My housekeeper was on vacation so I hired Brandy. My husband and I like to support local businesses, you know."

Ben Parker wasn't up for re-election for two years, but Heidi was already on the campaign. I guess it's never too early to start, especially with his personality.

"Oh, I know," I replied. "So you hired Brandy?"

"Yes. They were scheduled to come twice while Amanda was gone. The first time, Brandy came with two girls. They did an adequate job, but the second time, she sent someone else with two other girls. After they left, I discovered my diamond bracelet was missing."

I tried to look horrified, but I had seen Heidi's bracelet. It was an expensive looking piece of jewelry but gaudy and way too large for her thin wrist.

"That's terrible," I said dutifully.

"Yes. I was heartbroken. I immediately called Brandy and told her. Can you believe she had the gall to say I had probably misplaced it?" She stopped briefly, still offended. "Anyway, I told her that if I didn't get it back, I was going to sue."

"Did you get it back?"

"No. She brought me a check. Apologized and asked me not to file a complaint. She offered to clean my house herself for free the next time Amanda was gone."

"She brought you a check? To pay for the bracelet?"

"Yes. The bracelet was insured for $15,000, but she gave me a check for $18,000. For my troubles, she said."

Where did Brandy get $18,000? From what I had been able to determine, her business was doing well, but I found it hard to believe she had that much cash sitting around. Reed Hill wasn't that big. The number of people who would hire someone to clean their house had to be fairly limited. And Brandy wasn't the only cleaning service in town.

"I wouldn't think she had that kind of money," I murmured softly.

"I didn't think she did either," Heidi said. "I was surprised when she contacted me about it."

"When was this?"

"This past Monday. The bracelet went missing on Thursday

the week before. I called her that day. She called me on Monday and asked to come by. That's when she gave me the check."

That was the day before I found her. I didn't know the time of death, but Brandy had to have been killed sometime early Tuesday morning before I arrived on the scene. Although it was a rough neighborhood, someone would have reported it if she had been there on Monday too.

"Did she say where she got the money?" I asked Heidi.

"No. I know she'd been trying to get into cleaning commercial buildings. I don't think she had many contracts yet but…"

I looked at Heidi. She was fiddling with one of the rings on her finger. She glanced at me slyly. She knew something but wanted me to ask.

"But?"

She shrugged. "I doubt it matters, but I've seen her going into Antonio's after they were closed."

"You think she was cleaning Antonio's?" I asked Heidi.

"No. Sheila Burns has been cleaning the place for years, but Brandy was seen going into the restaurant many nights about an hour after closing."

"Why?"

Heidi let out an unladylike huff. "I don't know."

I asked Heidi about the other girls who had cleaned her house, but she didn't know any of their names. We talked a few more minutes. I quickly realized she didn't bother with anyone who couldn't help her cause. She believed many of the women were illegal. They could clean her house, but as they couldn't vote, she couldn't be bothered to learn their names.

I wondered what she would say if she knew my mother had been born in Mexico. My grandparents had come to the U.S. when my mother was about ten. They hadn't been illegal immigrants, but even today, my mother couldn't vote. She had never applied for citizenship. Heidi would have been shocked and dismayed if she knew. I was tempted to tell her just to see the look on her face. Instead, I thanked her for her time and walked out. I hadn't liked Heidi before my visit, and I liked her even less by the time I left.

It was almost one, and I was getting hungry. I didn't want a repeat of the day before so I forced myself to take a break. Most Saturdays I was working so I ate lunch at the store or in one of the restaurants on the square, but I decided to do something different. I called Olivia to see if she could join me at The Burger Coop.

Because I was supposed to be taking it easy, Olivia had helped open Scents and Sensibility. Once all three of my employees had arrived at the store, she had left it in their capable hands. She agreed to meet me with the caveat that two of her boys would be with her. I loved her kids so that wasn't a deal breaker for me.

The Burger Coop was a small restaurant on the south side of town. Most people would call it a hole in the wall. It had that feel. It had about fifteen tables tightly packed and a few booths on one wall. The lighting was poor, and the place was dingy, but the burgers were delicious.

I arrived first and secured us a table in the far corner near a window. Olivia, Billy, and Eric were only a few minutes behind. We placed our orders and settled in to eat. I talked to the boys for a while, catching up. I typically saw the kids two to three times a week. They often stopped by the store or my apartment with one of their parents, and I was usually at the Weston house at least once on the weekend, but I hadn't seen them for over a week. Olivia waited patiently, but once the boys were otherwise occupied, she pounced.

"Tell me everything. What have you learned?"

"Unfortunately, not much," I said and filled her in on my morning.

"So you still don't know what's up with Ricky or if he was even following you, but you now know that he, Damian, and Leon are back in the drug-dealing business. You haven't learned who would want Brandy dead, but you know she somehow came up with $18,000 to pay off Heidi."

"Well, yeah, I guess that about sums it up," I said dryly.

Olivia was a great listener, but she had no patience for drama. She always jumped right to the point.

She shrugged. "At least you have a clue."

"Mom. It's almost two," Billy said.

"Darn," Olivia said. "We have to go. Soccer practice. Leah, be careful."

Both boys gave me a hug, and in a matter of minutes, they were gone. I sat at the table checking my phone for messages and absently eating a few leftover fries. Griggs had returned my call, but when I tried calling him back, it went to voice mail again. I hadn't heard from Marcus and was thinking about calling him when the door of the restaurant opened.

Leon Hollins walked in. He was a huge man. Well over six feet tall and at least two hundred and fifty pounds. There were only a few tables occupied. He didn't look around but walked directly over to the last booth with several dirty dishes on the table and sat down. Leon pushed the dishes aside. Almost immediately, one of the busboys came over and started cleaning. Leon said a few words. The busboy replied and walked away. Leon rose, walked to the counter, and ordered a milkshake to go.

When he turned to leave, he saw me and froze. I was glad Olivia had already left. Leon had held her oldest son, Aaron, at gunpoint. If she had still been in the restaurant, all hell would have broken loose. It was about to anyway. I moved toward him with murder in my eyes. The man had threatened a child. A child I loved.

He ran for the door, and I was right on his heels. I might have even caught him if he wasn't a slimy weasel. He was just outside the door when I reached it. I pushed it open and was greeted with a milkshake to the face. It blinded me for a moment, and by the time I recovered, Leon had jumped in a car and sped away.

"Damn it!" I said, dripping chocolate ice cream. The only good thing that came from the incident was that I saw the car *and* the driver.

CHAPTER 14

After assuring the manager of The Burger Coop I was fine, I returned to my apartment to shower and change. On the way, I called Griggs. I was fuming when he answered.

"Not a good time, Leah," he said.

"I want to press charges against Leon Hollins. He attacked me!"

"Are you hurt? Where are you?"

His voice was full of worry so I quickly explained. There was a long pause. I waited impatiently. When I heard a soft snort, I almost screamed.

"Don't you dare laugh!"

"I'm not laughing," he said. Although I heard the trace of humor in his voice, it was gone, and something cold had replaced it when he spoke again. "I'll have a talk with Hollins. He won't bother you again."

It soothed the anger, and I relaxed a little. I was still furious with Leon, but I couldn't tell how much of that was because of the milkshake or left over from the gun episode. There was a lot of anger still simmering from the gun episode.

"I still want to press charges," I repeated.

Griggs sighed softly. "I guess you can, but he's likely to claim self-defense. By your own admission, you were chasing him."

"He shouldn't even be out of jail. He threatened Aaron and Myra. Held them at gunpoint."

"I know, Leah. It sucks. I agree. But he has a good lawyer and no criminal history. I'm not surprised the judge allowed bail."

"I hate him!"

"He'll get what's coming to him. When his case goes to trial, he'll serve time," Griggs said. "In the meantime, you should stay away from him."

"He needs to stay away from me," I muttered.

"Tell me about the busboy. Do you know him?"

I frowned as I pulled into the parking space in front of my apartment. Why was Griggs asking about the busboy? Sometimes I admit I'm a little slow to recognize something. This time I had an excuse. From the minute Leon had walked into the restaurant, I had been fighting my emotions. Now that I could think back without the haze of anger, I saw what Griggs had seen from the start.

"You think he was selling?" I asked.

"You tell me."

Leon went directly to a table covered with dirty dishes. All the other unoccupied tables had been clean. The table he chose was toward the back and in a corner. The dishes had been sitting there when I had walked in. It was the one table that hadn't been attended to immediately. And why sit down at all before placing a to-go order?

"Probably. He moved the dishes the busboy picked up. He could have easily deposited a small package on or near one of the plates."

"And the busboy scooped it up."

"I didn't see anything, but I'll bet that's exactly what happened."

"Do you know the busboy?"

"No. I don't think I've ever seen him before. I don't remember him working at The Burger Coop any other time I've been there. The manager didn't have him clean the table, and they weren't that busy. It was as if Leon was expected."

"Not much we can do at this point. I'll have my officers keep an eye on the place, but if Hollins and Ricky Cantono both saw you, they'll change the drop."

The car I had seen leaving had been driven by Ricky. It was more proof that the Cantonos were back in the drug business. I was sticky and uncomfortable. I was also getting tired. It wasn't as bad as it had been the day before, but I needed to rest. I ended my call with Griggs and went to clean up.

The shower and clean clothes helped my mood. I hated that I tired so easily but reminded myself it had only been two days since I was in the hospital. It had taken me almost a week to feel normal the last time I had a concussion, and this one was worse so I took an hour-long nap and woke refreshed.

It was too early to eat dinner, especially since I had had a late lunch, but I decided a glass of wine at Bella's was needed. If Marcus happened to be around, all the better. I wanted to talk to him about the vandalism again. See if I could get a few more details. If it was connected to Brandy's murder, that might narrow down the suspects.

The wine bar at Bella's was refined and elegant. It had subdued lighting and relaxed seating. There were several tables placed carefully around the room to maximize comfort. The bar itself was at the back of the room, and behind it, from floor to ceiling, were two large wine racks filled with bottles. They served hard liquor, but wine was their specialty.

When I walked in, I was surprised to see Megan Ross sitting alone at the bar. I settled on the stool next to her. She gave me a hasty look but immediately went back to nursing her drink. The bartender walked over. Most of the staff at Bella's knew me. Although I didn't come in often, when I did, it was usually to see Marcus so most of them quickly learned my name. I ordered a glass of chardonnay and asked if Marcus was working.

"No," Kyle said. "I haven't seen him today. I think Mike started his shift though."

"If you see him, would you tell him I'd like to speak with him?"

"Who?" Kyle asked with a smile. "Marcus or Mike."

I laughed. "Both. But Mike since he's here."

Kyle sat the wine in front of me, checked on another customer at the other end of the bar, and disappeared into the back. I took a sip and waited. I didn't want to drink much. It wasn't wise to mix alcohol with the painkillers. The wine was just an excuse to visit Bella's.

"Do you want to talk about it?" I asked softly.

"No," Megan replied.

"I'm sorry," I said.

"What?"

"I'm sorry. I told Griggs about you and Marcus."

She snorted. "I don't blame you. I blame me. I should've come clean. I won't be surprised if he fires me."

The last part came out on a choke. Megan swallowed and took a drink from the glass in front of her. It wasn't wine. It was something much stronger. Whiskey with two cubes of ice. She held it between both hands like a lifeline.

"He won't fire you," I said reassuringly and tried not to feel guilty.

"I was out of line. I should've told him."

"Maybe, but he won't fire you."

She didn't reply. We sat in silence for a few minutes. I couldn't think of anything to say to reassure her. Mike came out from the door behind the bar and glanced over at me. He gave me a grin and walked around the bar.

"Hey, Leah," Mike said as he slid onto the stool next to me.

"Hi, Mike. How's it going?"

"Good. Kyle said you wanted to talk to me?"

I was unsure how to approach the subject with Mike. He and his brother had been close. I didn't know if they still were, but they were family. If it had been Marcus, I would have just asked. In the end, that was all I could do anyway.

"Mike, do you know what's going on with Ricky?"

"What do you mean?"

"I think he was following me the other day. I've heard he's back selling."

Mike's face shut down. He looked away, but I saw the hurt in his eyes. When he turned back, his face was closed. "I don't know nothing about that."

He rose from the stool and quickly walked away without a backward glance. I didn't try to stop him. Mike had to know that if Ricky was selling, his father was involved. Although Mike was turning his life around and appeared to respect his uncle, he was still Damian's son.

"The Cantonos are selling again?" Megan asked, curiosity lining her voice.

"It looks that way," I replied. I told her everything I had learned from Sean and Dee and what I saw at The Burger Coop. Her mouth twitched, but she refrained from laughing when I mentioned the milkshake.

"Great. And I'm on suspension."

"Doesn't mean you can't help," I said softly.

She laughed humorlessly. "Griggs would have my ass if I got involved. He made it clear I needed to stay out of all police-related business until he caught the killer. I really screwed up. David's out sick, and there's no one else to take over a case that big. The chief has his hands full with the murder investigation."

"Don't you think they're related?"

A frown appeared on her face. "What do you mean?"

"Damian hates Marcus. He'll do anything to get out from under his control. Maybe even murder."

Megan shook her head. "Damian has an alibi. He was with Autumn."

"You don't think Autumn would lie for him?"

"Of course," Megan replied, "but at the time of Brandy's death, there was a disturbance at a neighbor's house. Damian was seen breaking up the fight. Witnesses said he came out of Autumn's house. His car had been in the driveway all night, and it took over an hour for the neighbors to calm down. It's possible he could have walked or stolen a car, but the timing doesn't work."

"Oh," I said, a little deflated. I wanted it to be Damian. "He could've gotten someone else to do it."

Megan nodded and took another drink. She motioned, and

Kyle quietly refilled her glass. "He could have, but we have no proof. Besides Brandy's murder—the whole setup. It's too subtle for Damian."

"Who else could it have been? Who else would've known Marcus's door was going to be unlocked? Was that just luck?"

"Shit. I'm surprised the whole town didn't know."

"What?"

Megan blushed. It was an odd look on her face. She was a beautiful woman but tough. She projected a hard, professional persona. I had never seen her blush. She glanced around the bar and shrugged.

"Don't know why I'm trying to be discreet. I told you that the night Brandy was killed I saw Marcus here."

"When you came to pick up a to-go order."

"Yes. Well, we talked. We hadn't seen each other for over a week. I had the flu and didn't want him around. The doctor had released me for work so Marcus thought that meant, well, you know."

"Sure," I said, trying hard to keep the humor out of my voice.

"He asked me to come over. We argued a little." She took a drink. "It was playful. I didn't think anything about it until he said he would leave the door unlocked for me. The place was busy. There was a party going on with a bunch of guys. It was loud. Marcus had to raise his voice to be heard. It was like a switch had been turned off at that exact moment, and everyone had stopped talking at the same time. The whole room heard him."

"Who all was here?"

"Oh, I don't know. A bunch of guys were celebrating Frank Garrison's promotion."

Frank Garrison worked for a high-tech company in Dallas. He was a local guy whose family still lived in Reed Hill. I didn't know Frank, but I knew his mother. I had heard he'd been offered a position with the company that required a move to New York. Rosalie Garrison wasn't happy about her son moving so far away, but that didn't stop her from bragging about his success. She told me about it twice.

"Frank doesn't live in town anymore. Why were they celebrating here?"

"The party was organized by a couple of his high school buddies, Warren Marsh and Curtis Wood. They invited a few guys from Frank's company, but the other two were also local, Glen Davis and Alan York."

I perked up a little. Warren Marsh had been one of the guys Brandy had recently dated. He had been all over her social media pages. Curtis Wood had appeared in her feed, but most of the time, he was with her and Warren. They were both on my list of people to contact.

"I'm surprised they had the party here and not at Antonio's if Glen was involved."

Megan motioned for another refill. Kyle topped off her glass and shot me a look. I had forgotten he was there, but he appeared to be hanging on every word. I don't know why I hadn't thought to talk to him. Bartenders hear everything. I raised my eyebrows. He smiled.

"Glen wasn't involved in the organization," Kyle said. "He and Warren never got along. Warren was always a little homophobic, and Glen has a chip on his shoulder. He wasn't openly gay in high school, but most of us knew. He and Alan didn't start dating until after high school. Frank, Warren, and Curtis had been good friends in school, but Frank was friends with Glen and Alan too. He kept in touch with all of them."

"Marcus told me he worked that night because the bartender had to leave early because he was sick. That wasn't you?"

Kyle shook his head. "No. That was Todd. He was supposed to work Frank's party while I prepared drinks for the patrons in the restaurant. Normally one person handles the bar, but Kevin knew the guys would be drinking a lot and needing more attention."

Kevin was the manager at Bella's. Marcus relied on him to run the day-to-day operations while he oversaw the marketing and long-term planning.

"Was there anyone else here that night?" I asked.

"A few people coming in to pick up to-go orders. Warren had reserved the bar area. It was closed to other patrons."

"Anyone picking up an order when Marcus opened his big mouth?" I asked.

Kyle laughed. Megan picked up her glass and drank half the contents. She slammed it back down on the bar. A little bit spilled out.

"Just that slut Autumn," Megan said, slurring her words. "She was coming in when I was going out."

"Autumn was here?" I asked. Megan didn't reply so I looked at Kyle. "She heard Marcus?"

He nodded. "Probably. She was meeting Damian. His shift was supposed to end at eight. She'd planned to sit in the bar while waiting for him, but Marcus made her leave."

Megan was right. The whole town probably knew about their relationship by now. I glanced at her. She was running her finger through the spilled whiskey from the glass which was empty again.

"Thanks, Kyle." I tossed a ten on the bar and took a deep breath. "Come on, Megan. It's time for you to go home."

CHAPTER 15

I managed to get Megan home without incident. She was drunk but not so drunk she couldn't give me her address. Luckily, she lived in a first floor apartment on Greenwood Avenue. I helped her into the apartment and onto her couch before looking around. Megan's home was much like the woman. Neat and tidy. It was decorated in soft shades of beige and blue. The couch looked comfortable and sturdy, and there was a lovely painting hanging on the wall above it.

Megan fell asleep the moment she hit the couch. I sat on the chair nearby. Any of the people in the wine bar on Monday night could have told someone else about overhearing Marcus, but I needed to narrow down the field. I ruled out Frank Garrison. He didn't live in town and had no stake in the restaurant business. The same with his friends from work.

Next were the other men in attendance. Warren Marsh and Curtis Wood were already on my list of people to interview. Warren had been the last man Brandy was dating. It's hard to tell from social media, but their relationship hadn't seemed very serious and hadn't lasted long. It was probably a dead-end, especially since I didn't know either of them or how to reach them.

Then there was Glen Davis and Alan York. Glen was in the restaurant business. He was an obvious suspect. Bella's had to be cutting into his business. Glen also had a little anger management problem. He had never become violent, but I had witnessed a couple of verbal altercations with customers and his employees.

According to Heidi, Brandy had been seen at Antonio's after hours so that was another a connection to Glen. He was married to Alan so in all likelihood he wasn't Brandy's boyfriend. I couldn't see why Glen would kill Brandy; however, I could see him as the saboteur. If that was the case, then the murder and the vandalism weren't related.

And finally, I couldn't forget about Damian and Ricky. They were up to their old ways. Marcus could and had interfered with that. Getting rid of him would clear their path and make it easier, although the police had to be watching them. I still believed I saw Ricky following me on Wednesday.

Megan started to snore softly. I quickly confiscated her car keys. Not because I thought she would try to drive, but because I didn't want to leave her car parked in Bella's parking lot overnight. It was a Saturday night, and the place would be busy. If I waited a few hours, she might be awake and sober enough to drive, but I had things to do.

To move her car, I needed help so I called Marcus. I hadn't heard from him since he had driven me home from the construction site. I hadn't tried to contact him because I was worried he might be a little put out that I had told Griggs about his relationship with Megan.

Marcus picked me up and drove me to Bella's. He didn't say anything to me about Griggs so I left that alone. I did tell him about seeing Ricky with Leon and about my conversation with Dee.

"Damn it. They never learn," he said.

"What are you going to do?"

He took a deep breath and shook his head. "Nothing. I've done all I can. I've offered both him and Damian a way out, but they don't want to take it. I'm done. Hopefully, they won't take Mike down with them."

"Do you think they will?"

He shrugged. "Mike seems to be doing okay, but it's hard to break away. I had to move all the way to California to do it."

Marcus had left Reed Hill with his wife and newborn son before I moved to town. He had not returned until his mother needed him. He worked at restaurants and attended college part-time until he had what he needed to start his own business. I never asked him exactly how he managed to do that.

"Is that why you left?"

"Yes," he replied. "Sam was just a baby, but Damian was already talking about how he and Ricky would be able to join the business. I realized I had to get my son out. I never brought him to visit because I didn't want to expose him to that lifestyle. It sucks you in."

"Smart of you."

"I had to protect him," he said quietly. He almost sounded scared. Marcus didn't talk about his son much, and I hadn't met Sam although he had visited a couple of times since Marcus moved back to Reed Hill.

I didn't have children, but I loved the Weston boys as if they were my own. I had several nieces and nephews, and I would do anything to protect them. I would imagine a parent would feel even stronger. Most parents, anyway. Damian only seemed to want to use his sons.

"Bet that went over well with Arabella," I said, trying to lighten the mood.

He laughed. "She wasn't happy about it, but she understood. Mama encouraged me to leave. She saw what was happening to Damian. I made sure she could visit us anytime she wanted. And Sam is now old enough and smart enough to make his own decisions. He took one look at Reed Hill at Christmas and told me he now understood why I fled."

"He wasn't impressed?" I said with a smile.

"He called it quaint."

"Now see, to me that's a compliment, but I guess to a twenty-year-old, it sounds like a death sentence."

"Something like that." Marcus stopped the car directly behind Megan's. The parking lot was already filling up. "I'm going to check in with Kevin before I head back over to

Megan's. It looks like we'll be busy tonight. I want to make sure all the staff showed for their shifts."

"I'll leave the car in her parking spot. Can you get into her apartment?"

His wicked smile appeared, and his eyes danced. "I don't have a key if that's what you're asking."

"That wasn't what I was asking. I was just wondering how you would get in."

"I'll knock, Leah."

"I guess that'll work. Hey, you said you didn't think the vandalism and Brandy's murder were connected. Are you sure?"

He ran his hand through his hair, the smile disappearing as quickly as it came. A frown formed between his brows, and his eyes searched the parking lot. It wasn't dark yet, but shadows were moving in.

"No," he said, "but it feels different."

"How?"

"The vandalism is aimed at closing the restaurant. We had reports of health violations, disabled cars so employees couldn't get to work, graffiti painted on the building, and the enclosure to the dumpster being nailed shut. All things that disrupted the running of the business. A health inspector could close the place down, or if we aren't providing enough staff or have an unsafe environment, people will stop coming. That could lead to a closure." He paused. "Brandy is different. If I go to prison for murder, the restaurant can still stay open. Kevin's a great manager who can easily run the place. His assistant and most of the employees are reliable, and Mama can oversee things."

"So killing Brandy is personal, and the vandalism is business."

"Maybe, but why Brandy? If you wanted to get to me by hurting someone, Brandy's way down on the list. I'm sorry she died. It's a tragedy. She didn't deserve that, but I haven't been involved with her for years. Haven't even had much contact with her. It just doesn't make sense."

"Griggs said you've been seen in her company a few times recently."

"She came by the restaurant a couple of times. We had a drink once. Another time she and a friend had dinner, and I stopped by their table. We'd been friends in high school, Leah. I didn't have much to say to her, but I wasn't going to ignore her either."

"Then it seems that framing you for her murder is more about getting rid of you than hurting you."

He snorted. "If I go to prison, it will hurt."

I hit him on the arm. "You know what I mean."

"Yeah. Maybe someone's trying to run me out of town."

"Something to think about anyway," I said and opened the door. "I'll talk to you later."

The drive back to Megan's apartment didn't take long. I parked her car in the assigned spot and used her keys to let myself back in. When I walked into the living room, Megan was awake but still lying on the couch. She looked at me a moment and then turned her head back to contemplating the ceiling.

"I brought your car back from Bella's," I said and tossed her keys on the coffee table.

"Thanks," she croaked. Her voice was no longer slurred, but she looked a little nauseous.

"You look like you could use a cup of coffee. Would you like me to make you some?"

She didn't move except to wave her hand in the general direction of the kitchen. I took that to mean yes so I set my purse on a chair and walked away. Like the rest of the place, Megan's kitchen was neat and tidy. She had a fancy coffee maker. I stared at it in envy before fiddling with the controls. I popped in a random pod and waited while it filled the mug. I then made myself a cup of delicious sounding cinnamon roll coffee.

When I returned to the living room, she was sitting up on the couch. I handed her the mug and settled on the other end. Silence reigned while we drank. The cinnamon roll flavored coffee was delicious.

"Did you say you brought my car home?" Megan eventually asked.

"Yep. I had Marcus pick me up from here, and I drove your car back. He said he would be by later to check on you."

"He needs to stay away."

"Why?"

"The chief told me to stay out of it. I don't want to lose my job. I've worked hard to get to captain."

Studying my mug, I spoke softly. "Did Griggs say to stay out of the murder investigation or to stay away from Marcus?"

Turning her head to the side, Megan was silent a moment. "He told me I couldn't investigate Brandy's murder because of my relationship with Marcus. He suspended me until the investigation is closed."

"The murder investigation, right?"

"Yes," she said, sounding confused.

"What about the investigation into the vandalism?"

"I assigned that to Luke Snyder. He's one of the more experienced officers we have, and he's training Cisneros. It'll be a good experience for him." She paused. "Why?"

"No one seems to think the two cases are connected. Do you?"

"No," she replied then paused. "It's certainly possible we have a murderer who freelances as a saboteur, but I think it's something else."

"What?"

"There's been a lot of resentment toward Marcus because of the success of Bella's. And not solely from other restaurant owners. Some people in this town have long memories. They don't want to see a Cantono succeed."

"So you think someone is trying to shut down Bella's just for spite?"

She shrugged. "Or for profit. He did take a lot of business from the other restaurants."

"Alan York told me Glen wanted to open another Antonio's location on the square. Antonio's has to be one of the restaurants most affected by Bella's. Do you think Glen could be behind the vandalism?"

"Maybe," Megan said slowly. "He has a temper and a lot to lose. I'd heard The Donut Hut was closing. It would be a great location for Antonio's, but I wouldn't have thought Glen had enough money to open another place."

"The Donut Hut is closing?" I squeaked.

Megan gave me an amused look. I didn't eat at The Donut Hut often. Nora's sold pastries and breakfast items, and with it being next door to Scents and Sensibility, I usually ate breakfast there if I didn't eat at home. But every now and then, I would crave a good old-fashioned glazed donut.

"I hadn't heard that," I said sheepishly.

"Cops always know about donuts," Megan said in a deadpan tone.

I laughed briefly and took another sip of coffee. "Could you, maybe, work on the vandalism case? It would allow you to still work—just not be involved with the murder investigation."

Megan shook her head. "The suspension was for not telling anyone I was involved with a suspect. If I'd come clean, the chief would've taken me off the murder case, but he wouldn't have suspended me. In a town this size, it's almost impossible for someone on the force not to know the suspects personally. Most of the time, it isn't a big deal. But petty crimes are one thing. Murder, that's different."

"If you aren't working either case, why does Marcus need to stay away?"

She opened her mouth and closed it again. She leaned forward and placed her coffee cup on the table. She picked up her keys, rose from the couch, and walked over to a table by the door. After tossing the keys into a wooden bowl, she turned back to me.

"Thanks for bringing the car back. I'm going to shower and go to bed early."

As a dismissal, it was pretty effective. Carefully, I placed my coffee mug on the table. I picked up my purse and walked to the door. Megan opened it.

"Goodnight," I said, stepping outside.

"Leah," she said softly. She wasn't looking at me when I turned around but staring over my shoulder. "Sabotage is one thing. Anyone could be doing that. Losing business is frightening. It affects our families and causes stress. But murder? Especially strangulation. That's something else. That's personal. Brandy was seen around Antonio's at odd hours. I wonder why?"

"You think..."

She shut the door before I could finish my sentence. Maybe I had been looking at this thing wrong. Everyone else seemed to think the vandalism wasn't connected to the murder. If that was true, there were at least two different culprits. So who wanted to shut Bella's down and who wanted Brandy dead? Both Megan and Heidi mentioned Antonio's. It was time for a visit. Good thing I was hungry.

CHAPTER 16

Antonio's was located on Market Street in a commercial district in the north part of town. It sat between Little Tykes Day Care and Carson's Automotive Repair and across the street from Walmart. The area was busy during the day, but at night, Antonio's and Walmart were the only places open. By the time I arrived, it was after seven thirty, and the parking lot was still full. I wasn't surprised because the lot was tiny. It only held six cars so there wasn't enough parking even when they weren't busy.

When there was an overflow, most people chose to park at the day care center or at Walmart. I preferred to park in the small shopping center that was on the other side of the vacant lot which was next to the auto shop. It was a longer walk, but I didn't have to cross a street.

As I parked the car, my phone rang. It was Griggs. When I had spoken to him a few hours earlier about the milkshake incident with Leon, he had told me he would be working all weekend. With David out sick and Megan on suspension, Griggs needed to be available. David was expected back on Monday, but for the weekend, Griggs was on call.

"Hey," I said.

"Where are you?" he asked in his deep rumble.

"Antonio's."

He was silent a moment. There was something odd in his voice when he spoke again. "We've already spoken with Robert and Glen."

So Griggs knew about Brandy being seen going into the restaurant late at night. If Megan knew, it had to be in the report. She had probably been the one to interview him.

"I'm hungry," I said truthfully.

"Uh huh," he said doubtfully. "Look, just be careful."

"You think someone might try to hurt me at Antonio's?"

"No, but something odd is going on there."

"What do you mean?"

"Robert was cagey when Megan interviewed him. She had a feeling he was withholding something. He gave some excuse about Brandy wanting to learn how to cook for a large group and had asked to use his kitchen. It was after hours so he didn't mind. He said he'd known Brandy's father and felt obligated to help her. Owen backed up his story. Said he was teaching her a few things."

Robert Davis was a nice man. He donated his time or provided food to all the community events and always sponsored one of the local sports teams. As a business owner, he knew a lot of people.

"That does sound like something he would do," I said cautiously.

"Yes, but Megan thought he was acting weird. She thought he might've been covering for someone."

"Protecting Brandy, you think?"

"Or someone else. Look, I shouldn't tell you this, but I know you are going to talk to him. He might open up more to you than he did with Megan." He paused. "Brandy was pregnant."

I gasped. "Are you kidding me?"

"No."

"That's so sad," I said softly. "Do you think that's why she was murdered?"

"Could be. Although she was only a few weeks along. It's unclear if she even knew. No one we interviewed has said anything about it. We'll have to go back and talk to everyone again and ask."

I thought a moment. "Does this hurt or help Marcus?"

"Cantono said the baby couldn't have been his. He's willing to provide a DNA sample to prove it."

"You didn't answer my question."

"That's because I don't know. Proving he wasn't the father will not exonerate him. He could've killed her because she slept with someone else."

"Do you think Robert might know who the father is? Did you ask him?"

"I haven't spoken to him yet. Megan didn't know about the pregnancy when she interviewed him. We only got the results from the autopsy this afternoon."

"Do I need to keep this information to myself?"

"We think Robert knows something. He isn't talking. I think that's because he knows who Brandy was involved with. I had planned on giving him the weekend to think about it before pushing harder." He paused again. "Don't tell him you heard about this from me, but maybe, you might've heard a rumor?"

I grinned. That was the closest Griggs would come to bending the law. He believed in the legal system even if it wasn't always just, but the one thing I had learned in the months that I had known him was that he would do everything he could to find justice for the victims.

We chatted a few more minutes before he ended the call with a reminder to be careful. I took a little more caution when exiting my car. The shopping center was deserted which was why it was a convenient place to park, but the lighting was sparse. I gave my car a quick pat and hurried down the sidewalk.

On Saturday nights, Antonio's was always busy. It was the perfect place for high school kids to hang out. They could pool their money, buy a few pizzas, and sit around. It was also a convenient stop for families on their way home after a hectic day of little league and soccer games.

When I walked in, it wasn't as full as I had anticipated. The teenagers had pulled a couple of tables together and were all congregated around them. It seemed like there were a lot of them, but I only counted eight. There were three families and one lone woman in a booth.

One of the families was a mother with two kids. Her youngest was the same age as Eric Weston. I often saw her at school events, but for the life of me, I could not remember her name. She waved, and I said hello.

The lone woman was Penelope Lansford. She gave me a brisk nod which I returned but didn't speak. I was surprised to see her at an establishment other than her own, but Glen walked over and sat down across from her. She must have agreed to meet with him and finally showed.

There was no line at the counter so I walked up to the cash register, and Robert greeted me with a shaky smile. Usually, Nathan, a local teenager, manned the cash register on the weekends. Miranda, Robert's full-time employee, worked during the week.

"Hi, Robert. No Nathan tonight?"

He tilted his head up and pointed his chin toward the teenagers. I turned to look. Nathan was sitting at the end of one of the tables quietly talking to a girl. He was still wearing his Antonio's employee t-shirt. All the kids were talking and laughing.

"With him working most Friday and Saturday nights," Robert said, "he doesn't get to spend much time with his friends. I told him to take a break since the rush was over."

"That was nice of you."

Robert shrugged and watched the kids with tired eyes. "Life's short. He needs to take joy when he finds it."

I frowned. The sadness in his voice was profound, but before I could speak, we were interrupted by Owen Miller. Owen was an interesting man. He had been working for Robert for as long as I had been in town. In his early forties, Owen was of average height and weight and somewhat stocky, but there was something extremely attractive about him. When he looked at you, it was as if you were the only person in the entire world. His rich brown eyes were mesmerizing, and he was a genuinely nice man. Most people have their own idea of what constitutes sex appeal, but everyone I knew agreed that Owen had it.

Normally, this would have made him quite popular with women, and he did get his fair share of dates, but Owen had a very mild intellectual disability. He finished high school but had trouble reading and writing. His speech pattern was different, and he was slow to respond sometimes. He was good at his job and a productive, functioning member of society. Sometimes it just took him a little while to catch up with everyone else. It wasn't obvious to the casual observer, but if you were around him for any length of time, it became noticeable.

He turned his beautiful eyes toward me and gave me a sweet smile. It drew me in, and I smiled back, my heartbeat speeding up just a little. He studied me for a moment. It was barely a pause but enough to be noted. Then his smile widened.

"Hi, Leah," he said.

"Hey, Owen. How's it going?"

"Good…Good." A short pause. "Pepperoni, mushrooms, and onions to go."

I laughed. "You know me well, Owen, but tonight I'm going to eat it here."

He smiled again. "Coming right up."

Robert handed me a glass to get a drink and took my payment. He said he would bring me the pizza as soon as it was ready. I wanted to question him, but another customer came in so I sat at the last booth on the far wall. This gave me a full view of the entire restaurant.

Glen rose from the booth where he had been speaking with Penelope. He said something sharp to her and walked away. Penelope just smirked. When she saw me watching, she quickly smoothed out her face. She rose, walked across the room, and out the door.

Glen watched her with a disgruntled look. As he passed my booth, I greeted him. Glen looked a lot like his father. He wasn't very tall, standing about five-nine. He had sandy blond hair and light brown eyes.

"Leah," he said stopping briefly.

"Penelope giving you a hard time?"

"Yeah. I don't understand her."

"You know, she can't stop you from purchasing The Donut Hut. She may be the president of the Downtown Business Association, but she can't dictate who opens a store."

"She can in this case. She owns it!"

"What? Penelope owns The Donut Hut?"

"Not the business. Just the building. She brought it last year."

Some of the businesses around the square rented their space while others purchased. For Scents and Sensibility, we rented for the first two years to make sure the shop would make it. After growing rapidly, we purchased the physical space. It was like owning a condominium or apartment. You shared walls, but the inside was yours.

"I didn't know that," I said.

Typically when one of the spaces on or near the square went up for sale, the whole world knew. The only reason we had been able to purchase our space was because Gabe's father knew the owner. He got a higher offer but still agreed to sell to us.

"No one knew," Glen said sharply. "She purchased all the spaces owned by the Viably Group."

The Viably Group owned four of the stores on the square. Their headquarters were in Houston, but they owned real estate all over Texas. Gabe, Olivia, and I had been hoping to purchase one of their slots for a couple of years. We wanted to move Scents and Sensibility onto the main square.

"How did we not hear about this?"

Glen's nostrils flared, and his mouth tightened. "They approached her when she was president of the business association the first time. I think they expected her to announce it to everyone, but she made them an offer, and they took it."

There was a crash from the kitchen. Glen cursed and stalked away while I was still trying to process the news. We had reelected Penelope as president because it was a hard, thankless job and no one else wanted it. She had been president for a couple of years, but one of the other shop owners agreed to do the job in January. Nora Gomez had lasted three months before giving up. Penelope agreed to take the position again. She did a good job. Although most people didn't like her, they respected her work ethic, but I never expected her to be so underhanded. I guess we got what we deserved by passing on the work. Penelope was in a position to take advantage of the situation, and she did.

I looked around. Glen had already disappeared. I wanted to ask him about Brandy, but I didn't see him in the kitchen. There was a small office at the back of the restaurant where Glen spent a lot of his time. He ran the business side of the restaurant while Robert dealt with the employees and customers.

I walked over to the counter. Robert was on the phone taking a to-go order so I stepped behind the counter and into the kitchen area. I didn't go any further. Owen was dishing up a plate of spaghetti. He looked up when I moved.

He frowned and cocked his head at me. "Pizza's almost ready, Leah."

"Great, but I was hoping to talk to Glen. Is he in the office?"

Owen looked around and then shrugged. "I don't know. I'll check."

He returned a few moments later shaking his head. "He isn't in there."

Puzzled, I blew out a breath. I hadn't seen him walk out the main door, and he wasn't in the restaurant, kitchen, or office.

"Do you think he left?"

"Maybe," Owen replied, "but he'll be back to help close."

Since Robert was still occupied and I couldn't speak to Glen, I decided to talk to Owen. According to Griggs, he had backed up Robert's story about Brandy.

"Owen," I said softly. "I heard Brandy had been coming by here after hours."

Owen froze. A panicked look crossed his face. He glanced toward Robert and swallowed. Then his face went blank.

"Brandy wanted to use the kitchen to learn to cook for a large group of people. We were helping her."

His voice was monotone, and the wording was carefully phrased. It sounded rehearsed. I studied him, but he didn't look me in the eye. Something was off. Just as Megan had noted. A buzzer sounded, causing both of us to jump.

"I have to get this," he said, turning to one of the ovens. "It's your pizza. You should go sit."

I slowly made my way back to the booth thinking about Owen. He had been in a long-term relationship when I first moved to town. I hadn't known Renee, but about the time we opened Scents and Sensibility, she received a job offer on the west coast. For a year, she and Owen tried a long-distance relationship, but eventually, they went their separate ways. Since then, Owen had dated quite a lot.

I leaned my head back on the seat. Could Owen be Brandy's secret boyfriend? I could see them dating. Owen had an appeal that was quite alluring, and Brandy dated a lot of different types of men. She had stated she was seeing someone in the restaurant business, but it didn't fit. Owen was a cook, but to say he was in the restaurant business was a stretch. Brandy had also indicated the man had money. Owen made a decent living, but he wasn't wealthy. Brandy hadn't been shy about posting pictures of all the other men in her life so why would they want to keep their relationship secret? Another question without an answer.

CHAPTER 17

"Here's your pizza," Robert said, sliding the pie onto the table in front of me.

"Thanks."

My stomach growled. The pizza smelled delicious. The crust was thick and lightly browned. The cheese bubbled, and the spices from the tomato sauce tickled my nose. I smiled at Robert. He nodded and started to turn away.

"Hey," I said. "Can you sit and visit a minute?"

The only people left in the place were a few of the high school kids and one of the families. Nathan was back behind the counter, and there was no one waiting for any orders. Owen was carrying dishes over to a sink, but Glen was still missing. Robert hesitated so I played on his sympathy.

"I'd like the company. I've been spending a lot of time alone or asleep because of the concussion. It would be nice to chat with someone other than my pets."

"Sure," he said, slipping into the booth. "I guess I can spare a few minutes."

"I heard Glen is looking to open another location," I said as I took a bite of the pizza. The flavors exploded in my mouth. I didn't moan, but it was a near thing.

Robert shook his head. "Is he still going on about that? I told him we can't afford it."

"Really?" I asked. "Are you losing business?"

"No. Well, we lost a little when Bella's opened, but not

enough to worry. We offer a different option."

"That's good. I was worried Bella's might have cut into your profit, but you're always busy." I paused to take another bite of the pizza. "You don't have enough business for another location?"

"Maybe. It would probably be okay once it opened, but we just don't have the money to invest in a new place anymore. I told Glen that when I gave…" He stopped. "I told him we didn't have the money now."

Up close, I got a better look at him. His eyes were red and puffy. His face was drawn, and he looked older than he did the last time I saw him. He looked heartbroken. Carefully, I sat the pizza back on the plate and took a drink of water.

"I'm sorry about Brandy," I said. Startled, he looked at me. I smiled. "I heard you were helping her. That you knew her father."

He nodded, looked away, and then back down at the table. He fidgeted with the checkered tablecloth, smoothing out the non-existent wrinkles.

"She…she was a good person. A beautiful woman." His voice was strained.

"How long had you two been seeing one another?" I asked quietly.

His head flew up. He stared at me with wide eyes. Shaking his head, he said, "I don't know what you're talking about."

"Robert," I chided gently.

He slumped into the booth. His hands trembled, and tears pooled in his eyes. My heart ached for him, but this was the reason Megan knew something was off. Robert had been prepared to speak with the police. He had his story in place, but I had caught him off guard.

"She was so pretty," he whispered desperately.

"Yes, she was," I agreed. "Robert, why didn't you tell the police?"

Wiping a hand across his face, he gaped at me in disbelief. "Tell them! They'd arrest me!"

"Why would they do that?"

"Leah, I'm sixty-four years old. Brandy wasn't forty yet. Only a few years older than my own son." He paused. "Glen called me an old fool. Said she was using me. Just after money. What would a beautiful young woman want with me?"

Brandy wanted stability and devotion. She also wanted someone with enough money so she wouldn't have to worry. Robert was still a good-looking man. He was kind and caring. I didn't believe she was with Robert merely for his money, but it was a factor. Glen was right about that.

"You're a good guy, Robert," I said. "I can see why Brandy would be attracted to you."

"You don't think she was simply with me for the money?"

"Do you have a lot of it?" I asked. Antonio's was successful, but Robert wasn't exceptionally wealthy, and he'd already said they couldn't afford to open another location. He shook his head. Blinking back tears, he kept his head turned away from the rest of the restaurant. I looked around, but no one was paying any attention to us. The kids were all engrossed with each other, and Nathan was on the phone. I saw Glen return to the kitchen. He glanced over at our booth, but he couldn't see his father's face.

"She needed money. Glen said it was the reason she was hanging around."

I sat up straighter. "You gave her the money to pay Heidi."

"That woman was going to ruin Brandy's business. A lawsuit would have cost Brandy everything. She promised to pay me back, but Glen…"

"Glen wanted the money to open another location."

"We've been saving a while. We had enough to put a down payment on a building, but the money I gave Brandy cut into our savings."

Things were all falling into place. Here were the answers to many of the questions. Of course, the biggest question was still unanswered.

"Robert, do you know who killed Brandy?"

Haunted, frightened eyes looked at me. He shook his head. I sighed. We sat in silence for a moment. Robert hadn't killed

Brandy. His grief was real, but the fact that he hid their relationship didn't look good.

"Did you see her on Monday?"

"In the morning. I met her here before we opened to give her the money to give to Heidi."

"But you didn't see her that night? She didn't stop by here Monday evening?"

Brandy died sometime after eleven thirty on Monday and before I found her on Tuesday morning. The police probably had a more specific time, but I had to guess. Marcus had said he arrived home after eleven and then went for a drive. The killer took his clothes while he was out.

"No. I didn't see her that night," Robert said. "I went straight home to bed. Like half the town, Miranda had the flu. She called in sick that night. Glen and Alan were at a party for Frank Garrison. We were really busy. It was lasagna night."

He gave me a tired smile. I nodded. Antonio's offered a discount on two of their specialties each week. Monday was lasagna, and Wednesday was fettuccine. Both nights, the place was always packed. Their specials were tremendously popular. I tried to hide my feelings of guilt. I used to come in most Wednesdays as I love fettuccine, but after I tasted the fettuccine at Bella's, I stopped eating Antonio's.

"So she didn't stop by?"

"No," Robert replied. He went on to tell me Glen and Alan arrived about an hour before closing. Robert had been so tired Glen had sent him home and stayed to close.

"Brandy didn't go to your house?"

His face reddened, and he dropped his chin. "No. No one knew about us. Other than the boys. We met here or at the lake. Brandy loved the lake. I have a nosy neighbor. If Brandy showed up at my house, the whole town would know."

"Why did it matter?"

"That's what she asked," he said with a soft sob. "I wish now I'd done things differently, but Glen and Alan reacted so badly when they found out. Even Owen didn't understand. You'd think in this day and age people wouldn't care who you loved. Especially Glen and Alan."

Everything I had learned about Brandy indicted she was a hard-working person but was looking for an easy way out of her lifestyle. I could understand why Glen might not approve. He probably hadn't been worried so much about the age difference but more about Brandy taking advantage of his father.

"You may be right," Robert said when I told him that. "Maybe it was more me. I didn't understand why such a young, vibrant woman would want to be with me. If no one knew about us, I wouldn't have to be embarrassed when she left me."

"What if she never left? Were you planning on keeping it a secret forever?"

"No. She'd enough of sneaking around. She thought it was fun at first, but she told me last week she wasn't going to do it anymore. We could go public, or we could break up."

"But you didn't."

"I was going to. I was going to take her to Arabella's birthday party. She was so excited about it."

Another piece to the puzzle. Brandy had posted about going to a private party at a new restaurant in town. I had thought it might be Arabella's birthday, but Marcus had not invited her so I had no idea whose guest she would be.

I watched the poor man sitting across from me. He looked broken. He brushed tears from his eyes before absently rubbing his chest over his heart. He looked at me with pain-filled eyes, and I wrestled with my conscience. Did Robert already know about the baby or would I be adding to his pain? Did it matter? He had a right to know. I just wished I wasn't the one who had to tell him.

"Robert," I said as gently as I could, "did you know Brandy was pregnant?"

Shock and despair warred on his face. The tears gathered and fell before the most horrible sound I had ever heard came from his throat. His head fell to the table.

"No. No. No," he cried.

Glen rushed around the counter and over to the booth. The teenagers stopped talking and stared at us. Owen stepped out of the kitchen and looked at me with troubled eyes. I didn't know what to say. I placed my hand on Robert's arm and waited.

"Dad!" Glen yelled. He turned an accusatory look on me. "What did you do?"

"Nothing. I…"

"Dad?" Glen sat in the booth and put his arm around Robert. "Dad! What is it? What's wrong?"

It was several minutes before Robert could speak. Glen glared at me from time to time, but I refused to say anything. If Robert wanted his son to know about the pregnancy, he could tell him. I wasn't going to be responsible for that news. I had already broken his heart.

When Robert raised his head, all semblance of the man I knew was gone. He was now nothing but a shell of his former self. I felt the tears running down my face. For a moment, the old Robert appeared when he saw my tears. He gave me a kind look and turned to his son.

"Brandy was pregnant," he croaked. "We were going to have a baby."

Glen stiffened. He sat back in the booth, glanced at me, and back at his father. He still had his arm around Robert and was blocking him from the rest of the restaurant.

"Dad," Glen began "Brandy was just coming by to use the…"

"No!" Robert said sharply. "No more lies. Leah knows the truth which means the police will know soon as well. Besides, I'm not ashamed. I loved her."

Glen's hand made a fist on the table. A vein throbbed on his forehead, and his eyes were bright and angry.

"That may be," he growled "but you don't have an alibi. That girl was pregnant. Everyone will think you killed her."

"You knew," I said.

"What?"

"You knew Brandy was going to have a baby. How did you

know?"

"Um. Dad said it."

I shook my head. Glen had been angry and upset when he sat down at the table. He was nervous and worried when Robert started talking, but he hadn't been surprised. He hadn't been surprised at all.

Robert regarded his son. "Glen?"

Glen huffed out a breath and leaned his head back. He didn't speak. The restaurant was quiet, but the patrons were no longer watching us. At least not overtly. I saw a few peek our way from time to time. The door opened, and a man walked to the counter. Nathan quickly stepped forward to take his order.

"Did you know?" Robert asked harshly. "Did you know and not tell me?"

"What would've been the point, Dad? She's gone." He glared at me. "All it would've done was cause you more grief."

"No. I had a right to know."

He sobbed softly. No one spoke for a moment. Robert's grief was intense. I could feel it, and Glen was affected by it too. We waited until the sobs subsided. I didn't want to cause him more pain, but I needed to finish it.

"How did you know?" I asked Glen.

He had been watching his father. At my question, he turned his searing gaze on me. He was so angry. I swallowed but didn't back down.

"If Robert didn't know, who told you, Glen?"

Robert looked at him. Glen rubbed his hand across his face. His mouth twisted bitterly.

"Brandy. She came by here that night."

"What?" Robert said. "I told you to tell her not to come."

"She didn't call, Dad," he said, exasperated. He looked at me. "She usually called the restaurant to make sure Dad was here before stopping by."

"But she didn't call Monday night?"

"No. She just showed up. I told her Dad had gone home early. She laughed. Said she would talk to him in the morning, but that I was going to be a big brother. She made me promise not to tell Dad before she could."

"Why didn't you tell me later?" Robert asked.

"Because you didn't need to know. It looks better if you don't know."

"Looks better!"

"Dad. You don't have an alibi. A woman twenty-five years younger than you is pregnant. She just weaseled $18,000 out of you. And the next day she turns up dead!"

"That's not what happened…" Robert whispered.

"But that's how it looks. You would be the police's prime suspect. They'll arrest you."

The door of the restaurant flew open, and two police officers walked in. I recognized both of them. The older one looked around, and when his eyes landed on our booth, he tapped the younger one on the shoulder. They began walking toward us. All conversations had stopped, and everyone watched.

"Oh my God," Robert muttered softly.

Glen took his father's hand as the two officers made their way through the room. They stopped beside us. The older one placed a hand on his gun which was in the holster on his hip. I watched Robert trembling and wondered what I could do to help.

"Ms. Norwood. Please step out of the booth."

CHAPTER 18

My jaw dropped as I stared at the two officers. Luke Snyder was the older one. He had recently been partnered with Keith Cisneros who had been on the police force for about a year. Keith was a local kid who had been the high school quarterback. I had known him for years although we seldom spoke to one another until he had been the first on the scene when I found the body of Isabel Meeks. It had been the first time either of us had seen a dead body. The incident had created an odd bond between us, and Keith often stopped by the store to chat. He treated me like an older sister.

Luke Snyder, on the other hand, had never warmed up to me. He was always polite the few times we met, but he was distant. I had the feeling he was suspicious of me. The look on his face reinforced that opinion.

"What?" I squeaked.

"Please step out of the booth."

I looked at Robert and Glen who looked back at me. Robert's eyes were wide and disbelieving, but Glen's face quickly transformed into a smirk. He raised one brow as if to say, *And you were questioning us?*

"Ms. Norwood," Snyder prompted.

"What?" I asked a little sharply. "What is going on?"

"We need to speak with you. Please step out of the booth."

I swallowed, picked up my purse, and stood. Snyder motioned for me to start walking. I glanced at Keith. He had an embarrassed look on his face and gave me a faint smile before turning to walk to the door. I followed with Snyder on my heels. The restaurant was silent as everyone watched our progress.

Once we were outside and the door had closed behind us, I turned to Snyder, eyes blazing. "What the hell is going on?"

He placed his hand on his gun again and glared at me. Keith shifted uneasily and moved next to me. Snyder turned his glare on his partner for a moment. Keith stilled but didn't back away. Snyder sneered, shook his head, and returned his eyes to me.

"We've had a report."

I crossed my arms over my chest and glared back. "What type of report?"

"An anonymous one. On our tip line. Saying you're the one responsible for the vandalism of Bella's restaurant, and we would find evidence of it in your car."

A laugh escaped me. It wasn't that I thought the situation was funny. It was disbelief. Incredulously, I asked, "And you believe that?"

"We take all tips seriously."

I rolled my eyes. "Why would I want to sabotage Bella's? What possible motive would there be?"

"Cantono dumped you," Snyder said. "You want revenge."

"Dumped me? We never dated! How could he dump me?"

Snyder just looked at me. "We need to search your car."

"Fine," I said with a huff and turned to walk down the sidewalk.

Along the way, I started to get a bad feeling. If someone went to the trouble of calling in a tip, wouldn't they want to be sure the police found something? I tried to remember if I had locked the car. My heart was racing, and my mouth was dry. By the time we reached my car, I was starting to hyperventilate. I took several deep breaths and forced myself to calm down. As Snyder was reaching for the door handle, I reacted.

"Wait," I yelled. He stopped and looked at me. I swallowed. "Do you have a search warrant?"

His eyes narrowed. "We have probable cause. We don't need a search warrant."

"I want to call my lawyer," I said, shaking.

"Be my guest," he replied while opening the door and looking in.

I pulled out my phone and looked for the number for Gloria Oakes. She was the corporate lawyer for Gabe's company and handled the few legal matters that were needed for our store. Gloria didn't practice criminal law but had studied it before switching to her specialty. The last time the police suspected me, Gloria had stepped in to help.

"Leah," Gloria said softly when she answered.

"Um. Hi," I said as I watched Snyder and Keith riffle through my back seat.

"Is something wrong?"

I pulled my eyes away from the car to concentrate on the call. Gloria was speaking quietly, and I could hear voices in the background.

"Sorry to bother you…"

"What's wrong?"

It didn't take long to brief Gloria. She asked a couple of questions but mainly listened. Just as I was finishing, the car doors shut, and Snyder walked around to the trunk. He reached for the release and popped it open. Leaning slightly, he rested one hand on the trunk door. It only took a moment before he turned to look at me.

With the phone still at my ear, I moved forward and looked in. Sitting in a cardboard box were several cans of spray paint and a toolbox. Snyder opened the toolbox to find a hammer and some long nails. He dug around a little and came up with a small string of flash firecrackers.

I sighed. The cardboard box was mine as was the toolbox and hammer. I keep those as well as a blanket and emergency kit in the box.

"We need you to come with us to the station," Snyder said.

"Am I under arrest?" I asked. I could hear Gloria calling my name. I told her what they had found.

"They can arrest you if you don't cooperate," she said. "Agree to meet them at the station. Tell them you'll follow them, or they can follow you. I'll be there as soon as possible. Don't say anything until I get there."

"I won't. Thanks."

An unnatural calm came over me. I told the officers what Gloria had suggested. Snyder didn't want to let me drive to the station on my own, but Keith prevailed. Snyder wasn't ready to arrest me officially so Keith got him to agree to follow my car. Keith smiled sympathetically as he grabbed the box from my trunk and took the evidence to the police car. Snyder gave me another dirty look before walking away.

The station was a few blocks away, but the drive seemed to take forever. All the while, I was trying to determine how the items ended up in my car. I was certain I had locked it before going to Antonio's, but the doors were unlocked when Snyder searched the car. Who wanted to set me up?

When we arrived at the station, I parked in the closest spot to the door. Snyder pulled their car into the spot next to mine. As I got out, I noticed Griggs's SUV in the parking lot. Relief ran through me. Griggs would help. He would know what I needed to do.

Obediently, I followed Snyder and Keith into the station. I had been there many times, but this felt different. All eyes followed us as Snyder led me to one of the integration rooms. My head kept turning toward the door to the chief's office, willing Griggs to step out, but the door remained shut. Keith peeled off with the box. I settled in one of the chairs, and Snyder sat opposite me.

"Why did you have paint cans in your trunk?" he asked.

"I'm not talking to you until my lawyer gets here," I replied.

"Eventually, you'll have to talk to us. Make it easy on yourself," he said softly. He gave me a fake smile. "Answer a few questions, and you can go. Where were you on the night of April 2?"

What happened April 2? I frowned but didn't reply. He snorted, rose from the chair, and walked out. I laid my head on the table and tried not to cry. I had been in worse situations, but this felt wrong. The last time I had been interrogated by the police, David Reddish had suspected me of murdering Isabel, but I never felt he was out to get me personally. He was doing his job. I was a suspect. That was it. He had questioned me, but he was professional. Snyder was a different story. I felt his resentment and anger.

I sat there alone and worried. My mind played through the events. I hadn't looked in the trunk of my car recently. The items the police found could've been in there for at least a week, but I didn't think that was the case. This was an act of opportunity. Someone had seen me in Antonio's and acted.

People had been coming and going all night. Several of the teenagers had left as had two of the families. Two or three other people had come in to place or pick up an order. I could remember most of them but quickly ruled them out. The person trying to frame me was probably the real saboteur, unless someone hated me enough to cause trouble, and I didn't know anyone who hated me that much.

So that narrowed the field to someone who had a grudge against Marcus and me. Maybe I had gotten a little too close with the questions I had been asking. I was trying to find out who killed Brandy, but if the saboteur and the murderer were the same person, I might have scared them into acting. It had to have been someone who saw me there and knew I wasn't going anywhere anytime soon. Two people came to mind. Penelope and Glen.

I wanted to blame Penelope, but Glen had a stronger motive. From what she had said at Thompson's Books, Penelope didn't like Marcus or anyone in the Cantono family, but what did she have against me? Unlike some of the other downtown merchants, I hadn't clashed with her. We weren't friends, but I didn't think she hated me.

Glen, on the other hand, had reason to resent both Marcus and me. Bella's had taken at least part of his business, and, even though the two restaurants offered different experiences, the food was similar, and I was helping Marcus.

I was still sitting there forty minutes later racking my brain for a suspect and going a little crazy when the door finally opened, and Gloria walked in. Gloria was a no-nonsense type of person. About ten years older than I, she didn't fit the friend category, and Gabe handled all the legal aspects so I didn't actually work with her. Mainly she was a person I knew who helped me out when I needed a lawyer.

She was in a cocktail dress with high heels and flashy jewelry. I stared a moment. She looked very different than the professional lawyer I normally saw. She was dressed for an evening out.

She took the chair next to me and looked at my face. "Are you all right?

"I interrupted your evening, didn't I?"

"Yes. Thank God," she said. My eyebrows lifted in surprise. She grinned. "I was at the most boring business dinner imaginable. Five financial management advisors and their spouses. And I thought lawyers were boring."

I laughed slightly. "Glad to be of help."

She glanced at her phone and sat it on the table. "Tell me everything."

I walked her through the evening, explaining why I was at Antonio's and what I learned. I needed to let Griggs know about Robert, but at the moment, I was more concerned about what was happening to me.

"So you think Glen might be setting you up?"

I shrugged. "I don't know. He doesn't seem the type. He has a temper, but I've never thought of him as underhanded. Everything is out there, you know. With Glen, he doesn't keep anything back, but he's the only one I know who had both motive and opportunity."

"What about the items in your trunk? Where those yours?"

"Some. The toolbox and hammer were mine. The nails in the toolbox weren't. They were long so I think they must have been like the ones used to nail the enclosure to the dumpster shut at Bella's. And the paint cans and firecrackers were definitely not mine."

Gloria's phone buzzed with a text. She read it and smiled. "Here's where we stand. Marcus Cantono has arrived and is telling the officers he will not be pressing charges against you."

I sat up straighter. "Marcus is here?"

She nodded. "Since he isn't going to press charges, the only thing the police have is the call to the health inspector. Technically filing a false report is a crime, but I pulled some strings and learned the caller who left the tip about Bella's was male. The police can't tie it to you."

"You did all of that in forty minutes?"

"I had help," she said with a laugh. "As soon as I got off the phone with you, I called Gabe. I told him to contact Mr. Cantono. And my sister-in-law works for the county. She knows all the local health inspectors. She called in a favor."

"I don't pay you enough."

"I told you last time. Corporate law is my specialty. It works for me, but I've always been interested in criminal law. I just don't want to represent criminals, and unfortunately, that's what a criminal lawyer has to do. You've allowed me to have a little fun without all the heartache."

"Once again, glad to help," I said sarcastically. Gloria merely grinned. "Does that mean I can go?"

"Probably. As soon as Mr. Cantono finishes talking to them, I'm sure you'll be told you can leave."

We waited another ten minutes before Keith opened the door and shot me a smile then rearranged his face into a more professional look. He thanked me for cooperating and said I was free to go. I wanted to ask him about Snyder, but he left before I had a chance.

When I walked out of the interrogation room, the whole station quieted. Olivia rushed over to me which caused the volume to return to normal. I got a glimpse of the room before she enveloped me in a hug, and all the officers were trying not to stare. Gabe was right behind her. He, too, gave me a hug and a quick kiss on the cheek. My eyes filled with tears that I had to blink back.

I thanked Gloria for her help as we turned to leave the

station. Griggs was standing in the doorway of his office talking to Luke Snyder. He glanced at me briefly before returning his attention to the officer. Griggs said something I couldn't hear, stepped back into his office, and closed the door.

A stab of pain shot through me. Did he believe I was guilty? Had Snyder convinced him I had been the one vandalizing Marcus's business? Griggs wouldn't normally take his officer's word over mine, but he had been worried about my relationship with Marcus. Did he really think Marcus dumped me, and I wanted revenge?

I shook my head and sealed away the hurt. Griggs would believe and do what he wanted. If he assumed I was guilty, then he wasn't the person I thought he was. My heart cracked a little more as I continued to fight back tears.

"Leah," Marcus called. He stopped in front of me. "Are you okay?"

I gave him a slight nod as we stood in the doorway of the police station. Gloria had already walked down the steps. I should've been happy. I was free and surrounded by my friends. Gabe stood to my left, Olivia to my right, and Marcus in front of me. Only there was no one standing at my back, and Griggs's door remained closed.

CHAPTER 19

Sunday dawned bright and clear. I laid in bed watching the shadows fade as daylight approached. Pandora was curled on the pillow beside me, and Harry slept peacefully on his bed in the corner of the room. I hadn't gotten any sleep. My mind raced as I tossed and turned. Each time I closed my eyes, all I could see was Griggs turning away.

It shouldn't hurt so much. We had only been dating a couple of months and hadn't spent that much time together. A few dates and hot kisses didn't make him indispensable. Our relationship wasn't even physical yet. So why did tears fill my eyes each time I thought about him? Disgusted with myself, I threw off the bed covers and went to shower.

When we had left the police station the night before, Gabe had insisted on driving me home. I had been too exhausted and hurt to argue. Olivia had driven my car, and once we were back at the apartment, my two friends had rallied around me. Gabe had taken Harry for a walk while Olivia made me some chamomile tea and forced me to eat a few crackers. I only had one slice of pizza at Antonio's, but I wasn't hungry. They finally left around eleven. I spent the rest of the night staring at the shadows and waiting for dawn.

I ate a piece of toast for breakfast as my stomach wasn't up for a full meal. Then I watched the clock, wondering if it was too early to start calling people. At eight, I gave up waiting and picked up my phone.

The first call was to Griggs. I had rehearsed what I was going to say all night so it was disappointing when I had to leave a message. I quickly told him Robert was Brandy's secret lover and probably the father of her child. I gave him my opinion about Robert—I didn't think he was the killer but simply a man afraid of what people would think. The message was short, and my voice was cool and impersonal. I didn't ask him to call me back. The more I thought about his behavior, the angrier I felt. And with me, that's not a good thing.

My next call was to Marcus to thank him for his help. He told me I wouldn't have needed help if I hadn't been trying to help him, and he told me to stop. I laughed. There was no humor in it as the anger had settled in my bones. Anger at Griggs, anger at whoever tried to frame me, and anger at the world in general. It was childish, but it made me feel better. If I wasn't angry, I had be in tears.

"Leah, we're worried. You've made yourself a target," Marcus said.

"I'm being targeted because of the sabotage, not the murder. Everyone keeps telling me the two aren't connected."

"What difference does that make?" he snapped. "You're still in danger because of me. You need to stop."

"Well, yeah, that's not going to happen," I replied and hung up.

The last call was to Gabe. Both he and Olivia would be checking up on me, and I wanted to head them off. Gabe was easier to fool than Olivia was. I thanked him for their help and asked him to tell Olivia I would be stopping by later in the day. The message would give me some breathing room and keep Olivia from tracking me down.

I still had a list of people from Brandy's social media pages I wanted to talk with, including Warren Marsh. Warren had been the last guy listed as being in a relationship with Brandy. His picture was all over Brandy's pages. He had also been at Bella's when Marcus had made the announcement that he would leave his door unlocked for Megan.

Warren had one social media page. Unlike Brandy, he didn't

post much. He mostly commented on or liked other people's posts. I couldn't find a physical address for him. He either had tight privacy settings or didn't have his name on any public records. In the end, I had to settle for sending him an online message. Surprisingly, he immediately replied and agreed to meet with me at two.

As it was still early, I took Harry for a long walk in the park and then bundled him into the car and headed out for the day. I had the whole morning free and a few errands to run. Sometime in the past crazy week, I had remembered to order a gift for Arabella.

After viewing her social media page, I learned Arabella loved to garden and cook. There had been a post referencing a certain herb she wanted to grow. Lovage was a culinary herb used in a lot of Eastern European dishes.

Arabella had mentioned she couldn't find the plant at any of the local home and garden stores. She had found some seeds but wanted the plant itself. It had been one simple online post, and she hadn't mentioned it again, but I hoped it would make a thoughtful gift. I did some research and found an online store that offered it. Unfortunately, they only shipped to nurseries. It took a little finagling and way too much money for one small plant, but I secured it and had it delivered to our local store.

Reed Hill Nursery and Garden Supply opened at ten and was located near the edge of town on Carpenter Street. It was a fairly basic nursery with a few varieties of trees and shrubbery. It did a little better with flowering plants and vegetables and had a small selection of tools. The building was a large barn-like structure with a sturdy roof and heavy plastic zippered walls that could be rolled open or closed as needed.

I had been there a couple of times. Without a yard, I was limited to house plants and already had several of those; however, when I started looking for a house, I visited the nursery to get some ideas of what to look for in a yard.

The drive took me along the freeway before I had to turn onto County Road 512 which ran west. About a mile down, there was a fork in the road. If you followed it to the left, you would eventually reach Fort Worth, but if you went right, it turned into Carpenter Street. There wasn't much traffic so it didn't take me long to arrive at the nursery.

Turning into the entrance, I noted the time. It wasn't ten yet, and the place was still deserted. The last time I had visited, there had been one employee working. It had been a Wednesday, and I was the only customer. Sundays should be busier, but I was one of the few people out and about. Most were at church or sleeping in.

I parked near the doorway, and Harry and I got out to walk along the short row of trees at the side of the building while we waited for the nursery to open. Most were no taller than I was and were still in pots or had their roots wrapped in burlap sacks.

My back was to the road when I heard a car. Turning slightly to look, I was startled when it suddenly gunned the engine. I quickly turned toward the street just in time to see the tail end of the car race around the corner, tires squealing, and disappear into a clump of trees. I caught a glimpse of the vehicle, and it looked familiar.

Another car pulled into the entrance and parked near mine. I was still trying to place the racing automobile when my phone rang. Glancing at the screen, I saw it was Griggs. My heart jumped, but I didn't know what I wanted to do. I was staring at the phone trying to decide whether to answer or not when I was interrupted by the young woman who had gotten out of the parked car. She was short and cute with light curly hair and a wide mouth. Dressed in jeans and a green t-shirt, she was full of life. Exactly the opposite of what I felt.

"Sorry. Are you waiting to get in?" she asked me as she hurried over. "I'm running a little late."

My phone had the time as exactly ten o'clock. I gave her a tired smile. "You're not late."

She grinned. "We're supposed to be ready for business at ten, but it was one of those mornings when everything went wrong, and I just couldn't get out of the house. Thankfully, we aren't usually busy until after lunch. Are you looking for anything in particular? I can point you in the right direction while I open up."

"I'm here to pick up an order that was delivered yesterday," I said, "but I'm not in a hurry. Take your time."

"Oh, you must be the one who ordered the lovage," she said.

"Yes."

"Great. I'm Tricia. Give me a couple of minutes, and I'll get it for you."

She opened the main door and waved me through. As Harry and I followed her in, she began unzipping the heavy plastic that made the walls. My phone buzzed indicating a message. I pressed my lips together and then jammed the phone into my pocket.

Tricia bustled around opening the place while Harry and I strolled through the aisles looking at the plants and smelling the flowers. It was going to be a warm day, but there was a light breeze blowing which felt wonderful. The place was quiet and peaceful. I could feel the tension from the previous night start to fall away. The birds were chirping and flying through the trees. There was a small bubbling water feature near the back. The flowing water created a relaxing atmosphere. Even the buzzing insects were soothing. Other than the sounds of the zippers and the rolling of plastic, the only things I heard were from nature. No people talking, no phones ringing, no cars driving by.

I stopped in the middle of one of the aisles. No cars driving by. I walked a little closer to the door and looked out at the road. At the edge of the nursery, it ended. The road curved to the left, but I couldn't see anything beyond it because of the large group of trees.

"Tricia," I said as she neared the register. "Do you get much traffic along this road?"

"No. Most cars are coming here. Or they're lost. Sometimes we get someone who stops and asks for directions."

"What's around the curve?"

"Nothing," she replied with a frown. "Well, I think there's an abandoned house somewhere behind the trees, but the road is a dead end."

So where was the car I saw earlier going? And more importantly, where was it now? I started to take a step outside to see if I could look around the bend, but Tricia called me over.

"Here's the lovage."

She held up a rather pitiful looking plant. It was in a small pot with a few stems shooting up. Each stem had about three leaves. It didn't look like a very nice birthday present. How was I going to wrap it?

"Don't worry," Tricia said with a smile. "It's hardy. This is typically the way a lot of herbs look when we first get them. Once it's planted in the ground or in a larger pot, it will be lovely."

"I hope so," I murmured as I paid for the plant.

A few minutes later, Harry and I were in the car. I had placed the plant on the floorboard in the back and wrapped a towel tightly around it to keep it from tipping over. I shook my head and hoped Arabella really did want the herb.

I backed out of the parking space and drove to the road. I paused a moment before turning right instead of left. Left would take me back to the freeway. Right took me to the curve in the road. I followed it. It wasn't long. I could see the end where the asphalt stopped and faded into the field. There was a gravel driveway on the right leading to an old, dilapidated house.

I slowed the car as I neared the driveway. Before I could turn in, another car shot out of a clump of trees and cut in front of me. Tires spewing up gravel, it raced around my car and back down the road. Stunned, I reacted instinctively. I executed a U-turn and stepped on the gas.

My car wasn't the fanciest on the road, but it was fast. I rounded the corner. The sound of something sliding across the trunk distracted me a moment. I glanced back at Harry. He was strapped in the dog seat belt harness. He barked once, and his tail wagged and flapped against the seat. I turned back to the front and saw the other vehicle speeding down Carpenter Street. I gunned the engine and followed. The other car wasn't as fast as mine, but the driver was more reckless. Mind churning, I increased my speed. The driver of the other car was Ricky Cantono.

It made sense now why I thought I had recognized the vehicle. I simply didn't understand why he had been following me. Thoughts ran through my head, but I quickly pushed them aside as I concentrated on controlling my automobile as it raced down the road.

The speed was getting dangerous, but I was beginning to gain ground when we reached the fork in the road. Instead of continuing straight onto County Road 512 which would have led us back into town, Ricky suddenly swerved to the right and made a sharp turn. Unable to keep the car in his lane, he moved directly into the path of a large pickup traveling west. The road had no shoulder lane so the driver had three choices. Risk a head-on crash, run off into the ditch, or turn onto Carpenter Street and into the oncoming traffic. He made the wrong choice.

I let out a scream as the pickup veered to the left, turned the corner, and barreled directly into my lane. I jerked the steering wheel and pulled us into the other lane just in time to miss a head-on crash, and Ricky was long gone. Shaking and wondering what the hell I was doing, I pulled back into the right-hand lane and slowed the car. Breathing deeply, I puttered my way back to town.

CHAPTER 20

"I'll take care of it," Marcus said. His voice was expressionless, but he was angry.

"How do you plan to do that?" I asked.

I was sitting at a patio table of a pet-friendly restaurant partaking of a late brunch. I had called Marcus to inform him about Ricky as soon as I sat down. Harry was asleep under the table after inhaling the treat offered by the staff. I was enjoying a leisurely meal consisting of a delicious mimosa—virgin and an order of eggs Benedict.

After the near crash with the pickup, I had pulled into a convenience store and turned off the car. It took me several minutes to stop shaking. All the while, I berated myself for being so reckless. Chasing after Ricky had been irresponsible and dangerous, not to mention stupid. Not only did I put myself in danger, but I also put Harry and anyone out on the road at risk. The worse part was I had no idea what would've happened if I had caught up with Ricky. I couldn't run him off the road. He wasn't going to pull over so I could question him. Was I going to ride his tail until he finally decided to stop? Like I said, stupid.

Once I had myself under control, I took a few minutes just to relax. I checked on Harry and Arabella's plant. Harry was unharmed. The lovage didn't fare quite as well. The towel had kept it from spilling everywhere, but it had lost some dirt and a couple of leaves. I scooped most of the dirt back into the pot and flattened the soil back down. I was beginning to think this gift was doomed.

Returning to my seat, I debated about what to do next. I still had almost three hours before I was to meet with Warren. The thought of sitting at home was unappealing. I didn't want to be inside. It was a beautiful day, and it wouldn't be long before it was too hot to spend much time outside.

When I pulled out my phone to check the weather, I was reminded that I hadn't listened to the message from Griggs. It was short. He thanked me for the information about Robert, told me they were short-handed, and he would try to call me later. No reference to the night before. He didn't even ask me how I was.

I didn't call him back. Instead, I called Olivia. My earlier call to Gabe had bought me some time, but I knew Olivia would be expecting to hear from me. My appetite had finally returned, and I needed to eat something. I told Olivia about my morning, omitting the car chase, and asked her to join me for brunch. It was unfair since I knew she would refuse.

Gabe and Olivia hosted lunch for friends and family on the first Sunday of each month. There were usually anywhere between ten and twenty people each month. We'd all bring side dishes, and if the weather was pleasant, Gabe would grill. Otherwise, Olivia cooked a ham or roast.

The other Sundays during the month, Gabe, Olivia, and their boys usually had lunch with Gabe's parents and his sister and her daughter. The elder Westons were great people, and I had an open invitation to join them anytime I wanted. I did occasionally, but large gatherings could be draining. With my job, I spent a lot of time with other people. I'm a people person and enjoy talking to everyone, but I needed the weekends to decompress. Olivia understood this and seldom pressured me about joining them.

My phone call reassured her I was fine and freed me up to find a meal on my own. Brunch at The Lake House in McKinney was the perfect spot. McKinney's lake was even smaller than Reed Hill's, but it was much nicer. It was in town so it was more like a city park than a recreational lake for boating. There were covered picnic areas, volleyball and horseshoe courts, paddleboats, and hiking and biking trails. It was beautiful. At one end sat an indoor/outdoor restaurant. It had a covered patio overlooking the lake, and they served a wonderful Sunday brunch. I didn't indulge often but always enjoyed it when I did.

"I intend to grab the brat by his scrawny little neck and force him to tell me what he's doing," Marcus said with a growl.

"Do you think he'll tell you?"

"You're damn right, he'll tell me. I'll make him tell me."

Marcus's words sounded harsh against the peaceful background. I applauded the sentiment. I wanted to know what Ricky was doing, but unlike Marcus, I wasn't so sure Ricky would be all that forthcoming.

"Well, good luck finding him."

"I don't need to find him. I know exactly where he'll be tonight at six o'clock."

"You don't think he'll skip out?"

"No. He wouldn't dare. He might mouth off to me or even his father, but he won't risk Damian's anger if he misses his grandmother's sixty-fifth birthday." He paused. "Don't worry, Leah. He'll talk."

"Okay."

"You're still coming, aren't you?"

"Of course. Looking forward to it."

Marcus reminded me of the time dinner would be served, and we said goodbye. Leaning back in my chair, I closed my eyes and raised my face to the sun for a moment before returning to my meal and enjoying the time to myself. It didn't last long.

McKinney was located about twenty miles from Reed Hill so I often saw people I knew at The Lake House. I wasn't surprised when two shadows appeared near my table and blocked out the sun. I looked up and saw a well-built Adonis. Trent Kearney was gorgeous. He had a charming, mischievous little boy persona and a flirty smile. He was a nice guy but very used to charming his way into getting what he wanted. He was basically the boy who never grew up.

With him was his wife of a few months. Jenny was the manager of Gemstones, a jewelry store on the square near Scents and Sensibility. She was the opposite of Trent. Jenny was quiet and serious. She had light brown hair and a pretty face but wasn't the type of person to turn heads. It had surprised us all when it came out the two of them had been dating and were going to have a baby.

Trent had been the object of Candace's obsession when she started killing anyone she thought was a threat to him back in December. After she learned Jenny was pregnant, Jenny became Candace's main target. I had stopped Candace from killing her, but it had been a near thing. Since then, Jenny and I had become friends.

"Hi, Leah," she said with a smile.

"Hey. What are you two doing here?"

"We come here every week for brunch."

"Oh, I've never seen you."

"It's a tradition. It's where we had our first date." Jenny glanced at Trent. He gave her a sweet smile. "We saw you once a couple of months ago, but you seemed engrossed in your book so we didn't interrupt."

It had been about two months since the last time I had come to The Lake House. I had probably been reading a book. I didn't remember, but that was what I usually did. I love reading murder mysteries. It was one of the things I had in common with Trent. He was a mystery buff too.

They stood there staring at me until I realized they were waiting for me to invite them to sit. I did, and they quickly accepted. The waitress hurried over and took their order. We chatted idly for a few minutes, but it was obvious they had something on their minds.

"Okay," Jenny said after their drinks arrived. "Trent needs to tell you something."

I looked at Trent. He bit his lip and looked down at the

table before he rubbed his hands up and down his thighs. Jenny elbowed him. He frowned and glanced at her.

"We talked about this," she said impatiently. "Tell her."

Trent was pleasant and handsome, but he was a little bit of a wuss. Jenny was definitely the dominant one in the relationship. It seemed to work for them.

"So, well, uh," he hemmed. Taking a breath, he looked around the restaurant and then leaned forward to whisper, "Ricky Cantono asked me about you."

I caught my breath. "Ricky? Why? What did he want to know?"

"Little things. Like what you did, where you spent your time, who were your friends. Things like that. He wanted to know where to find you."

"And you told him?" My voice was accusatory. I had put myself in danger to help him. It hurt that he would just throw me under the bus.

Trent's face flushed. He wouldn't look me in the eye. Jenny placed a hand on his arm before turning to me.

"Ricky threatened me—again."

During my search for Isabel's killer, the drug-dealing operation came to light. Trent had been forced to help Isabel run the merchandise through the store for the Cantono family and a corrupt police officer, Raymond Hunter. After Isabel's death, Damian Cantono had threatened Jenny to force Trent into taking Isabel's place. It hadn't lasted long, but Trent had been miserable. In the end, he told the police everything he knew and received a lesser charge. He was on probation but not facing any jail time.

"I just found out this morning," Jenny said. "I told Trent we weren't going to live like that again. We're going to report the threat to the police, but I wanted to make sure you knew."

"Thanks for that." I turned to Trent. "Do you know why he wanted to know about me?"

"Not really." Trent was starting to relax. He leaned back in his chair and reached for Jenny's hand. "I got the impression he was following you around. He made a comment about not getting paid if he lost you again."

How long had Ricky been following me? I had seen him a couple of times, but I hadn't been looking for a tail.

"He was getting paid to follow me?" I asked Trent.

"That's what it sounded like."

"Any idea why?"

"No. We're not exactly friends. When I questioned him about it, he clammed up and made a few threats." Trent paused. "I'm sorry I didn't tell you, Leah. This happened on Friday. I looked for you at work. I was hoping I could run into you and drop a hint without Ricky finding out."

Trent was back to working at Patina. When they reopened, Anthony Thorpe's daughter had needed someone who knew the business. She rehired Trent but kept a close eye on him.

The waitress returned with their food, and Jenny changed the subject. We spent an hour talking and eating. Harry had woken and proved to be a hit with the kids at a nearby table. It was a pleasant way to spend the time.

As we were preparing to leave, I saw another couple near the hostess stand. Glen Davis looked haggard, and Alan was hovering close. I debated about approaching them. Glen hadn't been happy with me when I spoke with his father, but I wanted to know how Robert was doing. The problem was solved for me when Alan saw me and smiled. I walked over, greeted them, and asked about Robert.

"He's devastated," Glen replied. "He went to the police this morning. Told them everything."

"That's probably good," I said gently.

"I know, but it was hard on him. He was so upset about Brandy he didn't even care if they arrested him."

"They didn't, did they?"

"No. He was home the night she was killed. Mrs. Hilton, who lives next door, told the police his car had been there all night. Thank God for nosy neighbors."

"So he's at home now?" I asked.

Alan nodded. "He wanted to be alone. We decided to give him a little space. We're here to pick up lunch. Robert loves

The Lake House's Quiche Lorraine."

"I'm sorry I upset him."

"I hadn't wanted to tell him about the baby. I knew it would make things worse." Glen grimaced. "That girl caused him so much heartache. I'm glad Cantono killed her."

Shocked, I reacted immediately. "Marcus didn't kill her."

"Oh, don't be naïve, Leah," Glen said. "Who else could it have been?"

"Gosh, I don't know. How about you?"

Glen jerked his head back as if I had slapped him. He stepped toward me threateningly. Sometimes my mouth got me in trouble. I probably shouldn't have said that, but I didn't stop.

"You have more of a motive. Brandy got Robert to give her $18,000 out of your nest egg. You thought she was demanding more from your dad, and then she became pregnant with his baby."

"It probably wasn't even his!"

"You don't think Robert was the father?"

"Who the hell knows? Brandy got around, you know. It could be anybody's. Even Marcus Cantono's."

Alan placed a hand on his arm. Glen shook it off and walked away. Alan turned to me. "Glen was home with me."

"He could have slipped out while you were asleep," I replied.

"No. He gets migraines. He was so upset about Brandy being pregnant. The stress brought one on. He doesn't like to take medication because the prescription the doctor gave him knocks him out. The one he had last Monday was so bad I didn't even have to talk him into taking a pill. He was out cold by eleven and didn't wake until late the next morning."

I didn't want to let Glen go as a suspect. He fit the profile perfectly. Alan would probably lie for him, but Griggs would have checked with the doctor to verify the medicine was prescribed and if Glen's reaction to it was possible.

"Leah," Alan said. "Glen didn't like Brandy, but he wouldn't have hurt her. He was more concerned about Brandy hurting Robert."

"Do you think she would have?"

"I don't know. I wasn't worried about it. Robert knew what he was doing. He knew Brandy's reputation, but he didn't care. He was having fun. I think that's why Glen was worried. Robert didn't seem to care what Brandy did or who she was with."

"She was unfaithful?" I asked, a little surprised. Brandy was a party girl, but I hadn't heard anything about her being with more than one man at a time.

Alan shrugged. "I don't know. I wouldn't be surprised. Glen's convinced the baby wasn't Robert's. It's one of the reasons he didn't want to tell his father Brandy was pregnant."

"The last guy she admitted to dating was Warren Marsh. I'm going to speak with him at two. Maybe he can shed some light on Brandy's personality."

"Your order's ready," the hostess said to Alan.

Alan said goodbye, and I watched him walk over to Glen who shot me a dirty look. I had made an enemy. Glen might not have killed Brandy, but he looked like he wanted to kill me.

CHAPTER 21

Warren Marsh lived in an apartment complex on the west side of town not far from Brandy's house. The complex needed a facelift. The buildings were old, and the paint was an odd color. Nothing looked out of code, but it wasn't the greatest place to live. The parking lot was torn up so maybe the management was working on sprucing up the place.

In the meantime, residents were parking along the street. Since it was Sunday, there were a lot of cars lining the curb. There wasn't a spot along the street in front of the complex so I turned onto a side road only to find cars parked there as well. About five cars down, there was an opening, but when I reached it, I discovered it was a fire zone.

With a sigh, I continued to the next block. There were no buildings on either side of the street. The lot was covered with tall grass and several trees which provided some shade. No one was around, and I didn't see any restrictions so I parked the car and got out.

I had planned to take Harry home before meeting Warren, but after Trent's revelation that Ricky had been paid to follow me, I changed my mind. I hadn't thought about being in danger, but I needed to remember someone out there was a murderer.

In February, Harry had bitten Leon when he broke into my apartment. He would protect me if he sensed I was being threatened. I also had my Glock as backup. It was reassuring to have it with me. People were surprised when they learned I not only knew how to shoot, but I was a crack shot. Having spent years training, I wasn't worried about hitting my target. As a final precaution, I sent a text to Olivia letting her know where I was. I couched it in a simple update so she wouldn't become alarmed and race to my rescue.

Harry and I walked down the street and around the corner to the complex entrance. Warren's apartment was near the front, and it didn't take long to find it. He must have been waiting for me because the door opened before I finished knocking. Warren was a good-looking man although he wasn't handsome like Marcus or Trent and didn't have the presence that Griggs did. His features were soft but pleasant, and his body was lanky and toned. He looked like a lot of other guys running around town.

"Hi," I said. "I'm Leah Norwood."

He offered me his hand. He didn't smile. "Warren Marsh."

"Nice to meet you. Sorry about the dog." I pointed to Harry. "We can talk outside if you want."

"No. It's fine. I like dogs. Come on in."

Harry and I stepped across the threshold and directly into the living room. There was a sturdy looking couch on one wall with a matching chair in the corner. A big screen television hung on the wall across from the couch. To the right of the living room was a kitchen with a small dining table and to the left was a hallway that I assumed led to the bedrooms.

A man was sitting on the couch, watching a baseball game. He reached for the remote and turned the television off before standing. He gave me a quick smile. I recognized his face from the pictures on Brandy's social media feed.

"This is Curtis Wood," Warren confirmed. "My roommate."

I hadn't realized Warren didn't live alone. He was in his mid-thirties, a few years younger than Brandy. I hadn't been able to find any address for Warren online. It could be he was just very careful, but I was betting it was Curtis's name on the lease.

"Can I get you anything?" Warren asked. His tone was even and polite but with a hint of anger running through it.

"No. Thanks. I just had brunch at The Lake House."

"I love that place," Curtis said.

"Me too." I gave him a nod and turned to Warren. "Thanks for meeting me. I wanted to talk to you about Brandy."

"No problem." Same tone, same inflection. "Have a seat."

I sat on one end of the couch, Warren on the other, and Curtis took the chair. Harry sat politely at my feet. It was awkward and uncomfortable.

"I don't know what I can tell you," Warren said. "I've already spoken with the police."

"I understand. I guess I want to know a little more about her. Her personality. Likes, dislikes. Things like that."

He studied me a moment. "Are you sure you're not just looking for a way to get Cantono off the hook?"

Unlike Glen, Warren's anger was somewhat hidden. I could see it in his eyes, but his face was devoid of emotion. He must have been one hell of a poker player.

"I don't believe Marcus had anything to do with Brandy's murder."

He laughed harshly. "Of course you don't. The two of you are tight."

My relationship with Marcus was well-known among my friends and business acquaintances, but I didn't know Warren, Curtis, or any other of the people involved in Brandy's life. I hadn't even known Brandy. It surprised me Warren knew enough about me to know I was friends with Marcus.

"You don't have to talk to me."

"Oh, I want to talk to you," he snarled, suddenly jumping to his feet, his anger no longer hidden. "I want to know what you've learned. I want to know why Marcus Cantono was cheating on her. I want to know why he isn't rotting in jail when all the evidence points to him!"

He was practically spitting by the time he finished speaking. Harry sat up and growled. I rose slowly and eased toward the door.

"I want to know why Brandy is dead!" he yelled.

Wild eyes turned to me. His face was red, his hands opening and closing into fists as sweat formed on his brow, and a vein throbbed at his temple. His was breathing heavily. I stopped, unsure if I should flee or hide.

"Warren," Curtis said softly.

The man froze. Warren's eyes closed, and he took several deep, gulping breaths. His whole body was clenched and shaking with anger. I slipped my hand into my purse and rested it on my gun. It took time, but he finally controlled himself. When his eyes opened, they were filled with so much pain I almost gasped.

"I just want to know why she's dead," he whispered, tears filling his eyes.

He had been in love with her. The pain and grief were evident on his face. Like Robert, Warren was devastated by Brandy's death. Unlike Robert, Warren's grief was wrapped in rage. I didn't know which was worse. Rage or regret. Both were heartbreaking.

"Then let me tell you what I know," I said gently.

He took another deep breath, unclenched his hands, and sank back down onto the couch, burying his head in his hands. I touched Harry lightly on the head and returned to my seat. I gave Warren another minute. He raised his head, took a drink of water from a bottle on the table, and nodded in my direction.

"We'll probably not agree about Marcus, but this is what I know."

Without betraying any confidences, I told them what I could. I didn't give them Robert's name. He had been at the police station so it wouldn't be long before that gossip made the rounds, but I wasn't going to be the one to start it. I didn't mention the baby. Warren was volatile. I didn't want to stir him up again.

After I finished, no one said anything for a few minutes. Warren was staring out a window. Curtis was leaning forward in the chair studying the carpet. He glanced at Warren then looked over at me.

"Then it wasn't Cantono," he said.

"Umm. I agree, but why do you say that?"

Warren rested his head on the couch and closed his eyes again. "Because Brandy would never cheat."

I must have looked perplexed because Curtis explained.

"Brandy's mother cheated on her father. A lot. She hated it. Hated her. Brandy was a flirt. She dated a lot of guys but always, only one guy at a time. If you have someone who admits to being with her, then she wasn't also seeing Cantono. Not unless the other person is lying."

"He isn't. There are others who back his story."

Curtis nodded. Warren was completely still. We sat there in silence for a moment. He finally raised his head and opened his eyes. The anger was still there, but the grief was in the forefront.

"I wanted it to be Cantono."

"Why?"

"He was her ideal man. She was always talking about how handsome he was, how successful, how he had made something of himself. The rest of us couldn't compete. She wanted someone who could take care of her." He stopped, looked around the apartment and over at his friend. "Hell. I can't even take care of myself. She broke up with me when I lost my last job and had to move in here with Curtis."

"So she was looking for a free ride?"

"No!" he said sharply. Curtis, too, was shaking his head. "It wasn't like that. She would work. Wanted to work, but she wanted stability. She wanted someone solid, you know?"

Robert Davis was exactly what Brandy wanted. I couldn't think of anything else to ask them. All I had wanted to know was if Warren could have killed her. Unless he was the best actor I ever saw, I had my answer. I thanked them for their time and headed to the door.

"The man she was seeing," Warren said softly from behind. "Did he do it? Did he kill her?"

I turned around. He was standing, watching me. I shook

my head. "No. He loved her."

I opened the door and walked out, closing it quietly behind me trying to shut out the grief. This case was getting to me. When I was looking into Isabel's murder, no one had liked her. I didn't have to deal with their pain. It was the same with Donnie. No one in Reed Hill knew him. It was easier to talk to people who weren't emotionally involved with the deceased. Brandy was different. People had loved her. My heart hurt for them.

Harry and I walked back out of the complex and down the street. My thoughts were so jumbled that I didn't notice anything out of the ordinary until I reached my car. It was covered with graffiti. Most of it was wavy lines and circles, but there were one or two choice words. All four tires had been slashed, and one of the windows was cracked. Someone had taken their anger out on my poor car.

Defeated, I sat down on the curb, buried my head in my arms, and cried. I was really tired of dealing with angry people. My head ached. The stitches along my hairline itched, and I was physically and emotionally drained. I no longer remembered why it was so important for me to find Brandy's killer. Marcus didn't need my help. He had one of the best defense attorneys in the state. Griggs admitted he didn't believe Marcus was guilty. No matter how he felt about me now, he wouldn't put an innocent man behind bars. I was putting myself in danger simply because I was curious and stubborn, but I was done.

Harry leaned against my leg and licked my arm. I raised my head. He looked at me so adoringly I had to smile. I kissed him on the nose. Wiping the tears from my face, I reached for my phone and called the police, a tow truck, and Myra. The tow truck was for the car, and Myra was for me. Gabe and Olivia would learn about the incident soon enough, but I just couldn't deal with their worry. Myra would come pick me up no questions asked.

A patrol car arrived with a couple of officers I didn't know. They introduced themselves as Officers Campbell and Pittman.

After I explained what had happened, they decided it was related to Marcus's case and called it in. I wasn't looking forward to speaking with Luke Snyder again, but I agreed with their assessment.

"The paint color's the same as what was used on Bella's," Snyder said when he and Keith Cisneros arrived. "Vandalizing your own car now?"

"No," I replied calmly. I wasn't going to get into a pissing match with him.

He looked at me a moment and snorted. Keith took pictures of the vehicle, and Snyder asked me a couple of questions. He didn't want to help, but he did his job. He recorded my statement and sent the other officers to Warren's apartment complex to ask if anyone saw anything. There wasn't much they could do, but I needed the report for my insurance.

"It's different," Keith said.

"What?" Snyder and I asked at the same time.

"The handwriting," Keith replied. "It's different from Bella's."

"It's paint," Snyder snipped. "You don't analyze handwriting on spray paint."

"Look." He pulled up a picture on his phone. I leaned over his shoulder and saw a door with 'Bella's Sucks' on it. "This is the back door at Bella's. See this letter here, how the bottom of the *B* curves down. It's the same every time."

He showed us a couple of more pictures, including one from the construction site in McKinney.

"How did you get that?" Snyder asked.

Keith ignored him and pointed at my car. "Now look at the *B* on Leah's car. It doesn't curve."

"Kid," Snyder said with a harsh laugh. "It's spray paint."

I studied the car. If Keith was correct, who had vandalized my car? I had assumed it was the saboteur, but I was looking for a murderer. This was another indication they weren't the same person.

"You think they're trying to make it look like it was the

same culprit?" I asked Keith.

He nodded. Snyder sneered.

"We have your report," he said to me. "We'll file it and let you know if anything develops."

He walked toward his car before turning back to us. "Cisneros, you coming?"

Keith shook his head. "I'll catch a ride back with Campbell and Pittman."

"Suit yourself."

Snyder got in the car and drove away. I turned to Keith. He was watching the car. When he saw me looking, he gave me a quick smile.

"Not very smart, antagonizing your partner," I said.

"I'm thinking about requesting a new partner," he said with a shrug. "Besides, he goes off on his own all the time. I'm going to work with the other guys on canvassing the complex. You okay here? Need a ride home?"

"No, thanks. I have to wait for the tow truck, and then Myra is coming to pick me up."

It took almost two hours for the tow truck to arrive. I rescued the lovage from the back seat and sent Myra a text while they hooked up my car. Myra arrived twenty minutes later and dropped us off at my apartment. I had less than forty minutes to wrap a plant, shower, dress, and drive across town to Bella's. I was going to be late.

CHAPTER 22

The parking lot at Bella's Fine Italian restaurant was half full. Considering this was a private party, I was surprised. How many people had been invited? I parked Olivia's car and hurried to the door. After Myra had dropped me off, I realized I didn't have any transportation. Olivia read me the riot act about endangering myself but eventually agreed to lend me her car.

Marcus had said to come around five thirty as they were serving dinner at six. It was two minutes before six when I arrived. The door was locked and had a sign stating they were closed for a private event. I cupped my hand on the glass and tried to peer inside. It was dark, but something moved, and a moment later, the door opened. Mike grinned at me.

"Cutting it close, Leah. You're the last one here."

"Sorry," I said. "Got held up."

He waved me in, and we walked to the main dining area. The place looked very different. Normally, there were tables for two or four all around the room, and the lighting was low to offer a refined, elegant dining experience. Now all the tables were pushed together to make two long rows with chairs on either side. There were colorful flowers on the tables and larger arrangements on stands in the corners. A happy birthday banner hung on one wall. Under the banner were two tables covered with presents.

Several people looked up as I stopped in the doorway but

most were chatting to each other or settling into their chairs. Waiters, carrying large trays with salads, started to serve those already seated. Arabella saw me and waved, her face filled with a bright smile. Marcus materialized in front of me looking handsome in his dark blue suit. He nodded to Mike who took my present and placed it on the gift table. Marcus took my arm, leading me to one of the few open seats near the end of the second row of tables. At least I was near the door.

"I was beginning to think you weren't going to make it," he said softly.

"Car trouble," I whispered.

"Everything okay?" he asked.

"Yes. Fine."

I didn't tell him about my car. It would upset him, and he had enough on his mind dealing with Arabella's party, Brandy's murder, and his relationship with a cop. I looked for Megan, but I didn't see her anywhere. Had she been invited or were they still trying to keep their relationship a secret?

"How did your talk with Ricky go?" I asked.

Marcus's mouth tightened. "I'll tell you about it after the party."

"In other words, not well."

"I was going to have you sit with Robert Davis," Marcus said, ignoring my comment, "but Glen called to say he wasn't feeling well. So you're on your own."

Marcus didn't know about Robert. I bit my lip, torn between letting him know who Brandy had been seeing and keeping Robert's confidence. In the end, I remained silent.

"Mama was pleased you were coming. She's looking forward to talking to you." He squeezed my arm and returned to his seat next to Arabella.

She was in the center of the table with one son on each side and her grandchildren across from her, including Ricky. He was dressed all in black. I couldn't see his face, but the set of his shoulders indicated he wasn't happy. Autumn was seated next to Damian, and there was a pretty girl in the chair beside Mike. The rest of the table was filled with other family members. I recognized a couple of Cantono cousins, and the woman sitting next to Marcus looked so much like Arabella that she had to be her sister.

As soon as I settled into my seat, a salad appeared in front of me. My dinner companions had already started eating so I joined in. The table where I was seated was for friends. Most of the people were around Arabella's age, but there were a couple of exceptions. Near the middle, there was a couple with two teenage girls, and the woman next to me had to be close to ninety. During the meal, I learned she was Arabella's first grade teacher.

"It was my second year teaching," she told me. "I was still learning the ropes."

"It's amazing that you kept in touch."

"I try to keep track of all my students. There are several here tonight. When you teach as long as I did, you have a lot of students."

"How long did you teach?"

"Forty years," she said with a laugh. "Oh, the stories I could tell."

With a little prompting, I got to spend the next hour listening to her stories. She was entertaining and fun. I was tired and fading fast so it helped that she kept me alert. At the end of the main course, Marcus stood and toasted his mother. We all raised our glasses in response. Arabella blushed prettily and clapped her hands.

"Time for presents," she said and hurried over to the gifts.

Mike followed his grandmother and set a chair near the table. Arabella sat and faced her guests. The woman I pegged as her sister joined Arabella. She was holding a notepad and pen. As Mike returned to the family table, I saw Ricky move toward the door.

Frowning, I glanced at Marcus. He watched Ricky a moment before he was distracted by one of the waiters. Damian shifted in his chair, staring at the doorway. My eyes followed his. Ricky was gone.

"My first gift is from Leah."

Crap. I twisted around in my seat to see Arabella holding my present and reading the card. I had tried tying a bow around the square pot, but the ribbon didn't look right. After some digging, I found a gift bag that was designed to hold a bottle of wine. The shape was perfect; however, the bag was too tall so I stuffed the bottom with tissue paper. It wasn't the prettiest present, but it worked.

Arabella reached in and pulled out the plant. The room was quiet with just a few people whispering. My gift drew a couple of puzzled looks. Arabella held the plant in both hands and looked at me. I couldn't tell what she was thinking. She wouldn't be rude, but I was getting a little worried about the look on her face.

"Lovage," she said softly. "I have been wanting this plant for months. Where did you find it?"

All eyes turned to me. "Uh. I ordered it online."

She laughed. "Of course. So simple. I should've thought of it myself, but now I don't have to. What a wonderful gift. Thank you, Leah. I love it."

"I'm glad," I said with a sigh of relief.

Arabella moved on to the other gifts. I watched her exclaim over clothing, perfume, and cookbooks. She was having a great time. I felt my eyes start to close. The day was catching up to me. Arabella was only halfway through the presents, and dessert still had to be served. I wasn't sure I was going to make it without falling asleep.

Deciding some fresh air might help, I rose from the chair and stepped into the lobby. The front door was still locked, but it wasn't hard to open. I slipped outside and took a deep breath of air. I walked a few steps along the front of the restaurant and turned around. Not wanting to leave the door unlocked without anyone nearby, I stayed close. After the third trip, I was starting to feel more awake.

As I neared the door, I heard a strange hissing sound. I stopped and looked around. The lights from the awning kept the area well-lit. I saw nothing out of the ordinary. Shaking my head, I reached for the door when I heard the sound again.

Walking to the end of the building, I looked around the side. It was empty, but the sound was louder. It was coming from the back of the restaurant. I continued to the back and leaned around the corner.

It was almost dark. The one light over the back door was faint. I could barely make out a man-sized shadow kneeling next to the door. His back was to me so I couldn't see his face, and he was dressed all in black. His arm started moving up and down, and I heard the ping of the small pea as he shook the spray paint can.

"Ricky," I muttered softly.

Anger infused me. He had been the one causing all this trouble. I rushed forward, calling his name. The shadow suddenly jumped up, turned around, and tossed the paint can aside. I skidded to a stop. He was wearing a black ski mask and was much larger than Ricky Cantono. I started to backpedal, but he reached out and grabbed me by the arm. Twisting me around so that he was behind me, he wrapped an arm around my body, pinning my arms to my sides. I let out a squeak and opened my mouth to scream as his hand moved to grasp me by the throat. He squeezed, cutting off all air.

Panicking, I started to thrash. With my arms now free, I reached up to tug at his wrist. He squeezed harder, holding me close. I struggled more, trying to break free. His other hand rose, and I saw the flash of a knife as it neared my face. I froze in place.

"You had to meddle in other people's business, didn't you? Nosy bitch."

Heart pounding and afraid to move, I said nothing. I could barely breathe and was in danger of fainting. Silently, I cursed the fact that my Glock was safely locked in Olivia's car with my purse. I felt him chuckle and tried to quash my panic.

"Let her go."

The voice came from the shadows. I almost sagged in relief until I saw Damian step into the light followed closely by Ricky. I didn't know which would be better. The unknown assailant or the two Cantonos who hated my guts.

The hand around my throat tightened, and I couldn't hold back a petrified gasp. My body was shaking all over. Even in the warm night air, I was cold. I couldn't seem to draw a breath. The hand loosened slightly, and I gulped in air.

"Let her go."

This time the voice was a welcomed one. Marcus stepped out from behind Damian. The two brothers stood side-by-side. They presented an intimidating image. The hand with the knife trembled just a tad.

"Cantonos joining forces? Never thought I'd lived to see the day," my assailant sneered.

With Marcus near, I was finally able to think through the terror. I recognized the voice. My eyes widened. I stared at Marcus, but his eyes were on the man behind me.

"You turned my boy against family," Damian said. The menace in his voice was chilling.

"Your boy jumped at the chance. Too bad he didn't do his job."

"I did what you wanted," Ricky yelled. Damian said something, and Ricky backed away muttering to himself.

"Ricky told us everything, Snyder," Marcus said.

The man stiffened. He hadn't expected to be recognized. I felt his breathing accelerate. Up until then, he had been calm and cool. I tried to control my own breathing, but I was still struggling with pulling air into my lungs.

"He doesn't know anything," Snyder growled.

"He knows enough. He knows Penelope Lansford hired him to follow Leah." Marcus paused. "Only Penelope wasn't the one vandalizing my business."

My brain was whirling. Nothing made sense. Snyder was the saboteur, but Penelope hired Ricky?

"For one," Marcus continued, "she isn't tall enough or strong enough. And two, she doesn't have the knowledge or expertise to circumvent my security cameras."

Marcus took a step closer. I never saw the knife move. When I felt it, I was so shocked I cried out. The cut wasn't deep, but it stung. I could feel a trickle of blood slide down my neck. Blackness threatened. Not from the pain, but from the fear.

"No closer, Cantono. Unless you want your girl here to lose an ear."

Marcus's eyes flashed to me for a moment before returning to Snyder. The smile that crossed his face almost made my knees buckle—and not for the normal reasons. The smile Marcus gave Snyder was cold and deadly. It reminded everyone that Marcus Cantono was not a man to cross.

"So we did a little digging," Marcus continued as if nothing had happened, but he had stopped moving. He slid his hands into his pants pockets and stood perfectly still. "Penelope Lansford is your cousin. You invested heavily in her restaurant. When her profits started to dwindle, she couldn't pay you. So you had two choices. Cut your losses or invest more hoping to recoup."

"It should've been a temporary setback," Snyder said harshly. "The newness of Bella's should've worn off by now."

"But it hasn't, and Penelope is up to her eyes in debt. She had overextended herself when she purchased the other stores on the square. The solution was to ruin my business."

"I guess you have it all figured out."

Snyder took a step back, pulling me with him. My feet shuffled on the ground as I tried to stay upright. We moved closer to the corner of the building. Marcus and the others were still near the door.

"Listen up, Cantono. I don't want to hurt Ms. Norwood." Snyder paused and then laughed. "Well, I do, but I'm a police officer and sworn to serve and protect. At one time, that actually meant something to me so this is how it's going to go down. Leah and I are going to get in her car and drive away. Once I'm sure no one is following, I'll let her go and disappear."

"If it had only been the vandalism, I would agree, but you killed Brandy."

Snyder's body shook. It took me a moment to realize he was laughing. I felt his head move back and forth as he huffed out a breath.

"No, that wasn't me. That was pure luck. Just another nail in your coffin."

My eyes met Marcus's. We both heard the truth in his voice. Marcus was still bound in place. He couldn't move without causing harm to me. I wasn't getting in a car with Snyder. He might have meant it when he said he would let me go, but I wasn't going to take that chance.

As Snyder took another step back trying to force me to move, I went completely limp. The momentum caused me to fall forward, pulling Snyder with me. I heard the knife clatter as he released it to reach for me. Before I fell on the ground, he let go and turned to run.

On hands and knees, I scrambled away. Behind me, there was shouting and running feet. I turned around and landed on my butt just in time to see Griggs tackle Snyder. Keith Cisneros was behind him. Griggs rose and planted a knee in Snyder's back while Keith stood over him with a gun.

"Leah!" Marcus grabbed my arm. "Are you okay?"

I nodded. "Yeah. I think so."

Griggs's eyes locked with mine. We stared at each other across the dark pavement. It was only a moment, but it felt like an eternity. And I didn't have a clue what it meant.

Snyder moved, causing Griggs to look away. He pulled out handcuffs and slapped them on Snyder's wrists. Keith reached down, and the two of them pulled the man to his feet and led him away.

I turned back to Marcus. "Do you think your mother would mind if I skipped dessert?"

CHAPTER 23

The following day I didn't arrive at work until almost noon. After Marcus assured me his mother would understand my leaving early, I had driven home, crawled into bed, and fell asleep before my head even hit the pillow. I slept for ten hours straight. Thankfully, Kara was scheduled to help Emma open the store so I only needed to be available for lunch breaks.

We were busier than we should have been for a Monday in April. I had found that intimately knowing about a crime was good for business. I enjoyed the increase in profits but wouldn't recommend it as a business model.

I spent two hours helping customers and answering questions. The questions I could answer anyway. There were still a lot of holes. It didn't matter to the gossips. They filled in the holes with theories of their own. As the news of Penelope and Snyder's involvement in the sabotage of Marcus's restaurants spread, sympathy for Marcus rose. For the first and probably only time, Marcus was being treated as one of our own. He had been the victim.

Midafternoon, Marcus called. He apologized for not informing me about their little sting operation and filled in some of the gaps. When he had confronted his nephew about following me, Ricky had clammed up. It had taken Damian to pry his tongue loose. The two brothers were both furious. Marcus, because Ricky had known about the vandalism and hadn't spoken up. Damian, because Ricky had betrayed family.

It turned out Damian hadn't been involved with trying to revive the family business. That had been all Ricky.

"Damian's mad at me and the world in general," Marcus said, "but he doesn't want to spend any more time in jail than he has to. He knows one more mark on his record will cause the upcoming court case to go badly. Right now, he has a chance of serving a short amount of time."

"But Ricky didn't agree?"

"Ricky is an idiot," Marcus said angrily. "He had no plan. Just got merchandise from a supplier and started selling. The problem was he had no base of operations. He tried selling out of Vanessa's trailer, and when she kicked him out, he tried to establish a drop at The Burger Coop."

"That could've worked."

"Sure. If you hadn't seen Leon. Ricky couldn't show his face there. He's too well-known so the idiot hired Leon."

"It was pure chance I was there at the same time."

"He should have recognized your car. He should've had a backup plan, but the stupid kid was desperate. He needed money. Fast. He was so desperate he applied for a job at The Reed Hill Café."

Penelope hadn't hired Ricky as a waiter, but she was worried enough about my snooping that she hired him to follow me. Penelope thought my search for Brandy's killer might shine a spotlight on the vandalism. Because Snyder had been in charge of the case, he had been able to control the information released by the police. Penelope believed I might accidentally stumble upon something that would point to them. She wanted to know everything I did, and everyone I spoke with.

After Ricky finally confessed his involvement, Marcus had contacted Griggs. Ricky was supposed to signal Snyder when all the party guests were occupied and keep the staff away from the back door. Marcus and Damian were going to confront Snyder and get him to admit to killing Brandy while Griggs and Keith Cisneros waited in the wings. It might have worked. Except for me.

No one had seen me walk out the front door. Marcus and Damian had followed Ricky to the kitchen. I had missed that when Arabella was opening my present. Griggs and his team were stationed at the back. When I confronted Snyder, everyone was surprised. Griggs and his team were about to come to my rescue when Marcus and Damian appeared. In the end, they had caught Snyder in the act, but he didn't confess to Brandy's murder.

"I *am* sorry, Leah," Marcus said.

"I'm not quite ready to forgive you, Marcus. I was in danger because you and Griggs decided to leave me out."

"We were trying to protect you."

"Really? And how did that work out?"

Marcus didn't have an answer. I made an excuse and ended the call. I would forgive him eventually, but I was still angry. Logically, I understood their reasoning, and I had no legal right to be involved, but it hurt that they didn't tell me about it.

I rubbed my hands across my face and neck, stopping when I reached the cut Snyder had given me. It wasn't much more than a scrape under my chin. I fingered it carefully and started shaking.

My life had been in danger before, but that night had felt different. Real. When Candace tried to kill me, she had been threatening Jenny. I had acted instinctively when I tried to tackle her and was able to fight for my life. With Wade, I had been more worried about Aaron and Myra. Wade had needed me to get him my great-grandmother's ring. He wasn't going to hurt me until he had what he wanted.

But with Snyder, I had felt helpless. The situation out of my control. Caught in his grip with the knife moving in and out of my sight, I had one of those moments when I realized I could actually die. It had terrified me.

Slowly, I pulled my hand away from my neck and took several deep breaths. I had survived. I had acted when needed. I wasn't helpless. I rubbed my temple, feeling a headache coming on. Reaching into my purse for some aspirin, I saw a crumpled piece of paper. I picked it up and smoothed it out. It was the list of people from Brandy's social media accounts. I stared at it. I was done. Isn't that what I had decided when I had been sitting on the side of the road next to my ruined car?

Autumn's name was at the top of the list followed by Heidi Parker. I picked up a pen and crossed off both of them. Next was Warren and his roommate, Curtis Wood. I ran a line across Warren. I hadn't really spoken with Curtis. He hadn't said much when I was speaking with Warren. Would he have anything more to add? I put an X next to his name. The final two names were Sherry Townsend and Hugh Olsen. I left them alone. I hadn't tried to contact them.

Tapping the pen on my desk, I allowed my mind to wander. Marcus had said Brandy's murder felt personal. Was it personal because of him or because of Brandy? Who would want to hurt him versus who would want Brandy dead?

I flipped the page over and started a new list with two columns. I filled out one column with people who might have killed Brandy to hurt Marcus. It consisted of Damian and Ricky Cantono, Penelope Lansford, Luke Snyder, and Glen Davis. Megan had mentioned that some people in town didn't want a Cantono to succeed, but there was no way I could determine who those people might be.

I crossed out Damian and Ricky. Damian had truly been upset when Ricky had betrayed Marcus. He was the type of person who would kick his brother when he was down, but no one else had better lay a hand on him, and while Ricky was trying to branch out on his own, he wasn't at the point where he would challenge Marcus.

I put an X next to Penelope and Snyder. Penelope hated Marcus. The problem was I couldn't think of any reason Brandy would agree to meet with her. She had been working with Snyder, but he had made it clear that Brandy's murder had been a lucky break for them. He could have been lying, but why?

Which left Glen Davis. Robert had admitted Bella's opening had cut into their profits. Glen wanted to open a second location, but that would be hard to do with Marcus still in business. Glen's name remained unmarked.

The other column was for people who might have wanted Brandy dead and framed Marcus because it was convenient. Heidi Decker, Warren Marsh, and Glen Davis. There were probably others, but no one else jumped out at me.

Heidi might have been upset enough with Brandy to kill her. Heidi's image was everything to her, and the loss of her signature bracelet could have made her snap, but in the end, she got paid handsomely for her troubles and got a great story to tell. I marked her out.

Warren had been in love with Brandy. He was hurting and angry, but his grief was real. When I had left his apartment, I had been convinced he hadn't killed her. Now I was second-guessing myself. He was truly angry. Was he angry with the murderer or Brandy? I put an *X* next to his name.

Once again, I was left with Glen Davis. Brandy had gotten money from Robert which had cut into Glen's savings. She was pregnant with Robert's baby which could have cut into any inheritance coming Glen's way. And he had been worried about her hurting his father.

Glen. He was on both lists. Everything pointed to Glen, but according to Alan, he had been out cold at home because of his migraine. Thinking about it was giving me a migraine. I took a couple of aspirin and laid my head down on my desk.

"Are things really that bad?"

Sitting back up, I turned my head. Griggs was standing in the doorway. He looked great. He must have been off work because he was dressed in jeans and a dark brown t-shirt which emphasized his beautiful green eyes.

My body started to relax. I felt an urge to walk over to him and allow his arms to wrap around me, but my mind resisted. It remembered him stepping back into his office and closing the door the last time I saw him.

"What are you doing here?" I asked.

"I'm here to see you."

He stepped into the office, closed the door behind him, and sat in the chair across from me. He studied me a moment, his eyes scanning my face before lingering briefly on the cut on my neck. His lips thinned.

"How are you?"

Unconsciously, I raised my hand to the cut. "Fine."

"I wouldn't have let him truly hurt you," he said softly.

"Yeah? Well, it would have been nice to know that sooner!"

He rubbed his hands across his face and huffed. "It was a police operation, Leah. We try not to involve civilians. The only reason the Cantonos were involved was because we needed Ricky to signal Snyder."

"All you or Marcus had to say was that you had something planned and to stay inside."

He snorted. "Like you would have listened."

"He could've killed me, Alex! He might have killed Brandy."

"He wouldn't have killed you," he growled. I could see the anger on his face. This was going to escalate into a full-blown fight. "I would have blown his head off before I would've let him cut you again. And he didn't kill Brandy!"

"Are you simply going to take his word for it?"

I don't know why I was antagonizing him. I didn't think Snyder was the killer either, but I was so angry and hurt that I kept pushing.

"Of course not. He was working the night Brandy was killed. The ME puts her death between three and five in the morning. Snyder was in the station with seven other cops including Cisneros."

That was that. You couldn't get a much more solid alibi. A few cops might have covered for his absence but not if he was accused of murder. I picked up my pen and crossed Snyder's name off my list. I stared down at the desk, not really seeing anything. The anger was fading, but the hurt remained.

"Leah?"

"Why are you here, Alex?"

"I wanted to see you," he said, sounding puzzled.

"So now that I'm not the saboteur you want to see me?"

"What the hell are you talking about?"

"I'm talking about Saturday night. I'm talking about you ignoring me."

"Are you kidding me? You're angry about that?"

"Yes," I shouted. "I'm angry about that. I was scared, Alex. I didn't know who was trying to frame me. All I knew was that Snyder was after me, and you wouldn't help."

He burst out of the chair and starting pacing. "I can't believe this. You actually think I didn't want to help you?"

"That's how it looked to me."

"Department policy is an officer cannot be involved in a case concerning someone they know personally. I had just suspended Ross for that very thing. There's a lot of resentment toward her, especially from Snyder. He had already filed an official complaint stating she should've been fired. If I had shown any involvement in your case, he would've gone over my head to the city council. I couldn't help you, Leah! It would have compromised the case and put you in more trouble."

I hated that he had a valid point. I hated that I couldn't let it go.

"Are you sure you aren't just mad about my friendship with Marcus?"

He sighed and sat back down. "I'm not mad about your friendship with Marcus. I don't think either of you realize how tight your connection is. Everyone sees it. Snyder even commented on it. Cantono would have killed Snyder for you. And you risked your life to help him."

Marcus would have killed Snyder if needed. I don't know if it would have been for me, but he had offered to have Candace killed so Griggs did have a point. I opened my mouth to respond, but Griggs held up his hand.

"Look, Leah. I know you and Cantono aren't romantically involved, but your attraction to each other is obvious to everyone."

"We kissed once," I said with a laugh. "It did nothing for either of us. No spark."

Griggs's shoulders relaxed a little, but he didn't respond. Marcus and I did flirt. He was that type of man—handsome and charming. I don't think he even realized he was doing it most of the time.

"That doesn't explain why I haven't heard from you for two days. You didn't even call to check on me after Saturday night."

"I did call you. You didn't answer. I told you in my message we were short-handed. Two more officers called in sick. Cisneros came to me with concerns about Snyder, and then I received the call from Cantono. My job isn't the nine-to-five version, Leah. I can't be there for every little thing."

That last sentence sounded bitter and harsh like something he had said before. I briefly wondered if he was really talking to me. Griggs and I hadn't shared much about our past relationships, but it couldn't be easy for a police officer to have one.

The door of the office suddenly opened. Kara walked in and stopped abruptly. She glanced at Griggs, at me, and back at Griggs. She gave him a tentative smile.

"Oh. Hi, Chief."

"Hi, Kara. How are you?"

"Good, thanks. Uh, Leah, it's four. Is it…"

"Of course. Sorry. Go. And good luck."

Kara was meeting her fiancé to look at a possible venue for their wedding. She gave me a big smile, gathered her things, and left. I rose from the chair.

"I need to get back to the floor," I said.

Griggs rose. He walked over to me. "Are we okay?"

"I don't know," I said with a shrug.

He nodded and kissed me on the forehead. "I'll call you tomorrow."

I stood in the doorway of my office and watched him walk away.

CHAPTER 24

The next two days passed slowly, and life returned to normal. Penelope was never arrested. Since she didn't participate in the vandalism, she hadn't done anything illegal. Griggs tried to get her on conspiracy charges, but Snyder refused to implicate her. We were all surprised about that until Penelope sold the café and her four storefronts to an anonymous buyer. The sale went through almost instantly because the buyer paid cash, and the next day a fancy defense lawyer from Dallas came to town. It appeared Snyder was willing to keep Penelope out of the case as long as she paid his legal fees. Either way, Penelope was finished in Reed Hill and left town the day after Snyder's arrest.

Griggs and I were talking, but things were strained between us. My feelings had been hurt. Probably more than they should have been for the offense. It worried me because it meant I cared for him even more than I had thought. I was in deep and didn't know if he felt the same.

On Wednesday morning, we had an emergency meeting of the Downtown Business Association to vote for a new president. With Penelope gone, we needed someone to take her place. No one volunteered for the job so one of the store owners nominated me. I was feeling a little guilty because it was my snooping that had brought Penelope's antics to light. After some arm-twisting, I agreed to finish her term which was until the end of the year. I immediately regretted it.

Griggs heard about the meeting. He stopped by the store and took me to lunch where I voiced all my frustrations. He was a good listener and didn't once tell me it was my own fault.

"Okay," I said, sitting back in my chair. "I'm done venting."

He smiled. "I don't mind. I understand the need to vent."

"What do you need to vent about?"

"Nothing," he said with a shake of his head.

"Come on, Alex. You listened to me."

"While you were meeting with the business association, I was meeting with the mayor."

"Ugh. What'd he want?"

Griggs paused. "He wanted to know why I hadn't arrested Marcus Cantono for Brandy's murder."

Automatically, I opened my mouth to defend Marcus but stopped. Griggs didn't need a reminder. He hadn't arrested Marcus so he must still believe he was innocent.

"What did you tell him?" I asked instead.

"I told him the same damn thing I've been telling him all along. We don't have proof. All the evidence is circumstantial."

"How did he take it?"

"Not well, but there isn't much he can do about it unless he fires me. And he can't do that without approval from the city council."

"I'm sorry."

He shrugged. "At least he okayed me lifting Megan's suspension."

"That's good."

"Yeah. I told him five days of unpaid leave was enough especially since we've been so short-handed. I haven't had consecutive days off in over a month. She'll be back tomorrow, and David's back from sick leave so I'm taking the entire weekend."

I laughed. "What are you going to do with all your free time?"

"I was thinking we could go somewhere."

"We?"

He nodded but continued eating as if he hadn't just

dropped a bombshell into the conversation. I took a sip of my tea and tried to think of something to say. He finally looked up.

"Don't you think it's time we take this relationship to the next level? See if we even want to be together?"

Slowly, I wiped my mouth with my napkin and set it down. I knew I wanted to be with Griggs. I was still a little angry and hurt, but that was more about my pride than anything else.

"Where would we go?" I asked softly.

"I thought maybe Austin or San Antonio since we only have a couple of days. Do you think you can leave early on Friday?"

"Yes, I can do that. I vote for Austin. It's closer so we'll have a little more time, and they usually have a lot of things going on."

He smiled. I smiled back. The rest of lunch was easy and relaxed. We quit tiptoeing around each other and went back to the comfortable relationship we had before our fight.

I returned to the store excited about our trip and ready to rearrange the schedule. I had been out several days the week before and didn't know what plans my employees had, but I was willing to close Scents and Sensibility if needed.

When I walked through the store, I heard a couple of women whispering. I heard one of them mention Marcus. I shook my head. Once the excitement of Snyder's arrest and Penelope's departure cooled, people remembered there had been a murder. The mayor wasn't the only one who considered Marcus the prime suspect. Once again, he was persona non grata. The construction at Bella's II moved forward, but patronage at the restaurant in Reed Hill fell off. He told me he wasn't worried. He got plenty of customers from those passing through town, but I could tell it was an issue, which meant I couldn't stop looking for Brandy's murderer.

I had spoken with both Sherry Townsend and Hugh Olsen the previous day, but Curtis Wood had been out of town. Neither Sherry nor Hugh had much to add. Brandy was a party girl who always had a good time. They both agreed she was a hard worker but wanted to settle down with someone who would take care of her. They didn't know anyone who would want her dead.

Glen was still my main suspect, but I didn't know how to approach him. He wasn't happy with me. I upset his father and accused him of murder. I needed a reason to visit Antonio's that wouldn't make me look like I was spying on him.

Curtis gave me one. He had returned to town. I didn't want to talk to him with Warren present so I offered to buy him dinner at Antonio's. Wednesday night was fettuccine night. It would be busy, and no one would notice two more people. Curtis agreed, and we arranged to meet at seven.

This time I parked in the Walmart parking lot. It was well-lit and had security cameras. I was driving a rental car while mine was getting a new paint job. Hopefully, no one would vandalize this one.

Curtis had already arrived and was waiting for me at one of the tables. I asked him what he wanted and placed our order before sitting down. We talked about the weather and other mundane things while we waited for our food.

"I know you want to ask me about Warren's relationship with Brandy," Curtis said as our food arrived.

I looked up to thank the server and did a double take.

"Alan?" I said. "What are you doing here?"

He gave me a smile. "Helping out. Robert needed to get away. He has gone to visit his sister. Most of the time, Glen and Miranda can handle things without Robert, but not on one of the specialty nights."

"The place is usually packed on Mondays and Wednesdays," I agreed.

He nodded and pointed to my glass. "You want a refill?"

"I can get it."

"It's no problem. All I'm doing is delivering food." He picked up my glass and walked away. He stopped by the counter and briefly spoke with Glen who glared in my direction.

I turned back to Curtis. "I don't want to put you on the

spot, but I did want to know more about Warren and Brandy. He seemed…I don't know…angry?"

"Mad as hell is probably better. He loved her so much." Curtis stopped a moment. "He was angry enough to do it, but he didn't. Warren was passed out drunk that night. We had a going-away party for a friend. Warren overdid it. There's no way he had the coordination to get up, drive to Brandy's, and kill her."

I sat back with a sigh. The suspects were dwindling fast. No wonder Griggs was frustrated. When Alan returned with my drink, I thanked him absently.

"Why are you still trying to find out who killed her? Cantono hasn't been arrested," Curtis said.

"No, but everyone thinks it was him. I'm not going to stop asking questions. Marcus didn't do it. Besides, there are several people who need closure. Including Warren."

"Well, good luck."

We finished our meal mostly in silence. It was a little awkward since we didn't know each other and didn't have much in common. Curtis was done before I was. He thanked me for the meal and left. I watched him, wondering if I should've asked him where he was the night Brandy was killed. He defended Warren loyally.

Curtis's chair wasn't empty long. Glen abruptly appeared and sat down. He glared at me then looked around the room. When his eyes returned to mine, I had to force myself not to move. I would have jumped from my chair if Alan hadn't moved to stand behind him.

"What are you doing here?" he growled.

"Umm. Eating dinner."

"Look, Leah. You broke my father's heart. You accused me of murder. You're not welcome here."

"Now wait a…"

"No," he snarled. "I don't want to see you in here again."

Alan placed a hand on his shoulder. "Why don't you return up front? I'll walk Leah out."

Glen shook the hand off and stood up. "I thought you

were going home."

"I am," Alan told him. "I'll see you there."

Glen stomped off, and Alan turned to me. He offered me his hand. I took it and got up. Once again, I felt as if I was doing the walk of shame out of Antonio's.

"Sorry about that," Alan said as he opened the door. We stepped through, and he closed it behind us. "Glen is under a lot of stress."

"Aren't we all?" I muttered under my breath. "I'll see you later, Alan."

"Leah? Do you have a minute?"

All I wanted was to go home, but Alan had been nice to me. I pasted a smile on my face as I answered in the affirmation. He smiled back.

"Great. I need to show you something. I think Robert may be suicidal. He wrote this odd note. I didn't want Glen to see it so it's in my car. Will you look at it?"

"Note?" I asked while following him to the back of the restaurant.

Alan was a tall man, and his strides were much longer than mine. He had disappeared behind the building while I was still trying to decipher his statement. I hurried to catch up.

The blow came as I rounded the corner. He hit me on the side of the head. I fell back against the wall, striking my head and seeing stars. I slid to the ground woozy and in danger of blacking out.

"I am sorry about this, Leah," Alan said in his soothing voice. "I always liked you."

He reached down and picked me up. I tried to struggle, but my head was spinning, and I couldn't think. I passed out for a few minutes. By the time I came to, Alan had my hands tied behind my back, a cloth gag in my mouth, and was loading me in the trunk. He tossed my purse in behind me.

"Be right back. I have to go establish my alibi."

The trunk shut with a soft click. I gasped for breath, trying not to panic. My head was pounding, and tears were running down my face from both the pain and the fear. My whole body started shaking, and I was close to passing out again. I forced myself to breathe through my nose all the while wondering how I was going to get out of this.

I tried to free my wrists, but he had used a plastic tie. Another wave of dizziness caused me to lay my head down. It landed on my purse, and my pulse accelerated. I had my purse. Once the dizziness stopped, I wiggled slowly, trying to force the purse closer to my hands. I had to stop twice because I became light-headed, but eventually, I was able to reach one of the straps.

I pulled the purse down to my hands and started digging. I left the gun alone. It wouldn't do me any good with my hands behind my back. Instead, I searched for my phone. I tried to hurry as I didn't know how long Alan would be gone, but I was moving sluggishly. When I felt my phone, I almost cried in relief.

I took several deep breaths, twisted my head toward my back, lifted my arms as high as I could, and tilted my hands up. Pressing the button, the phone lit up. I squinted trying to see the screen. It was dark, my eyesight was blurry, and the angle made it almost impossible to see the phone. I tried to remember which side the emergency option was on the screen. I tapped one of them, and the phone keypad appeared. I could only see the top part of it. I had to turn the phone upside down to see the nine. I pressed it and turned the phone back up to reach the one.

The car door opened and shut. Alan had returned. He started the engine. I twisted the phone upside down again, looking for the dial button. I reached for it just as Alan put the car in gear and stepped on the gas. The phone flew from my hands, and I banged the front of my head against the tailgate, not knowing if the call went through.

I slipped in and out of consciousness as we drove through town. Lying as still as possible to reduce the nausea and pain, I lost track of time. I had no idea how long we had been driving when the car came to a stop.

The trunk popped open, but I didn't move. As difficult as it was, I kept my eyes closed. I was going to need all my energy and strength. Alan picked me up. I remained still. When he turned and took a step, I jerked and thrashed. The movement caused him to drop me, and I fell to the ground.

"Now, Leah, don't be difficult."

I tried to scream, but the gag muffled the sound. I had landed on my back so I quickly sat up and tried to scramble away. With my arms behind me, movement was difficult, but I was strongly motivated. Alan sighed heavily. As he stepped closer, I kicked out. He grunted when I connected with his leg. He bent over, and I tried again. He grabbed my foot, holding it in place. Still leaning forward, he reached for me. I pulled my other foot back and thrust forward. I was aiming for his stomach to push him away from me, but he leaned back at the last minute, and my foot connected a little lower.

Alan cried out. He released me, bending over and covering his groin. It took several tries, but I finally rose to my feet. Swaying, I looked around. We were at the lake. Alan had parked as close to the docks as possible. If I could make it to the street, I might have a chance. I had just started across the parking lot when he grabbed me from behind.

"Fine. We'll do this the hard way."

In the distance, I heard sirens. I hoped they were for me. Alan's hands seized my arms and started pulling. I lost my footing as he dragged me across the pavement to the grass. I tried to slow him down by kicking and twisting, but it wasn't long before we reached the dock. I bent my heel on the short step. It stopped him momentarily, but he gave one hard jerk. My shoe flew off, and I sobbed in pain as the wood scraped the back of my heel.

Time was running out. He continued to drag me across the dock. I tried to hook my leg around a post, but they were too short. When we reached the end of the walkway, Alan pulled me up to my feet, lifted me up a little, and started to toss me off the dock. My wrists were tied, but my hands and legs were free. I grasped the front Alan's pants and wrapped my legs around his. I saw the flashing lights of the police cars just as we hit the water.

CHAPTER 25

The ceiling tiles were square and pitted. I sighed and closed my eyes again. I immediately reopened them. I was alive. The world was blurry, and my head pounded, but I was alive. A blob moved into my line of vision and gradually came into focus.

"We have to stop meeting like this," the friendly nurse said quietly. The room was dark and cold. "If you're not careful, we'll have to give you a frequent visitor's card."

"God, I hope not," I slurred.

Shivering, I raised my hand toward my head and winced. It hurt. Everything hurt. My head, my wrists, my legs. My eyelids wouldn't stay open. The nurse added another blanket to the bed as sleep claimed me once more.

The next time I woke the room was lighter. A small sliver of sunlight peeked through the blinds. I had a moment of déjà vu when I saw Olivia was sitting in a chair reading a book.

"This is becoming a habit," I croaked.

Olivia looked up, snapped her book shut, and frowned. "Unfortunately."

"Sorry, Liv."

Her face softened. She rose and helped me sit up before offering me a drink of water. My throat was scratchy, and my entire body ached. There were bruises forming along my wrists, and I could feel a bandage on the back of my heel. Slowly, I touched my head. No new bandages, but one side of my face was swollen. I patted my hair.

"They didn't have to cut any," Olivia said with a laugh. "Do you think you could eat something? The nurse brought you some scrambled eggs and chicken broth."

I made a face but dutifully ate the eggs and swallowed a little of the broth. It satisfied Olivia. She moved the rolling tray table away from the bed. I laid my head back on the pillows just as the door opened, and Griggs walked in.

He looked exhausted. His color was off, and his eyes were rimmed in red. He gave me a tired smile. Olivia picked up the breakfast tray and slipped out of the room.

"Hey," he said, coming to sit by the bed.

"Hi."

"How are you feeling?"

"Honestly? Terrible. Everything hurts." I paused. "But I'm glad I'm able to hurt."

"Yeah. That was a little too close." He ran his hands briskly across his face.

"What about you? You look tired."

"I didn't get much sleep. David interviewed Alan, but I wanted to listen. We also had to talk to Glen. It took hours."

"So did Alan kill Brandy or was he covering for Glen?"

"It was all Alan. Glen was home drugged to the gills. He had taken a pill for his migraine, and Alan slipped sleeping powder in the water. Between the two, Glen was out cold."

"Alan admitted that?"

"Alan admitted everything. He sat there calmly telling us everything in that soothing voice of his. It was creepy as hell."

"Can you tell me what he said?"

Griggs nodded and leaned back in the chair. "He claimed it was all for Glen."

In the weeks leading up to Brandy's murder, Glen had grown more and more agitated. He was worried about his father's relationship with Brandy and Bella's effect on their business. He became obsessed with opening a second location. The night Brandy announced she was pregnant she had taunted Glen.

"According to Alan, she said she knew Marcus Cantono personally and was going to get him to buyout Robert so he could retire early and help her with the baby."

"Marcus isn't interested in Antonio's," I said.

"No, but Glen didn't know that. It was the last straw for him. He flew into a rage, yelling and throwing things. Brandy left, leaving Alan to pick up the pieces." Griggs reached for the pitcher on the night stand and poured a cup of water. He took a deep swallow before continuing. "Alan said he drove Glen home and gave him the sleeping powder. Once Glen was out, he picked up Cantono's clothes. Early in the morning, he contacted Brandy and told her Robert was ill and asking for her."

"It wasn't on her phone records?"

"There was a call that morning to her cell. It was from one of the few pay phones still left in town. Right around the block from Brandy's house."

"So when she came out to get in her pickup, Alan was waiting."

"Yup. He's the one who hit you in the back of the head at the lake and vandalized your car. You told him you were going to find out who killed Brandy. He believed you."

I grimaced. "I guess I need to stop doing that. You'd think after this many murders I'd recognize a killer."

Griggs shook his head. "Only a few people actually look and act like a murderer."

I leaned back against the pillows. "I feel like I could sleep for a week."

"Me, too."

"Sorry about Austin."

"Austin isn't going anywhere. We'll try again."

I smiled. "Do you think they'll let me out? I'm really growing to hate this place."

"I'll see what I can do," he said, getting up.

I closed my eyes and fell asleep. I wasn't out long because when I woke, Griggs was talking quietly with the nurse who was handing him several sheets of paper. She smiled at me.

"Good. You're awake. Dr. Pater has released you. You're to see your own physician on Monday." I nodded. "In the meantime, you need someone to stay with you. Our good chief here has volunteered for the job."

I raised a brow but didn't say anything. I just wanted to go home. I signed my name a couple of times and then I was bundled into a wheelchair while Griggs went to get his car. Before I knew it, I was sitting in his front seat.

"Do you mind if we stay at my place?" Griggs asked.

"What about Pandora and Harry?"

"They're both with the Westons. Olivia said she would stay at your apartment if you preferred, but we thought it would be better for the animals to stay with the kids so you can get some rest."

I was so tired I couldn't even think. "Whatever works best."

Griggs turned left and headed toward downtown. We passed the square and turned onto Ash. When we drove by my apartment, I stirred.

"Where are we going?"

"My place," he said in a puzzled voice.

"But you live the other way."

He laughed. "That's right. You haven't seen my new house."

With a sinking feeling, I fell silent. Griggs turned onto Park and pulled into the driveway of the little Cape Cod house. I blinked back tears. He had purchased my dream home. Griggs was the one who stole it from me.

"I grabbed this place the minute it came on the market. It was exactly what I was looking for," he said as he opened his door and got out. He walked around the car to open my door. "Can you walk?"

I nodded and slowly got out of the car. Griggs reached into the back and pulled out an overnight bag. I recognized it as mine. Olivia must have put it together for me. I took a step and swayed a little. Griggs dropped the bag and reached for my arm.

"Okay?" he asked.

His hand felt clammy. I looked at him. His face was flushed, and he had his other hand on his stomach.

"Are *you* okay?"

"My stomach's a little upset. I've been living on fast food and items out of the vending machine."

I touch his forehead. "You're a little hot."

"I'm just tired. Let's get you inside."

He picked up the bag, and we both moved slowly toward the house. I was breathing heavily by the time we reached the bedroom. I didn't even look around. All I wanted was to crawl into bed. When Griggs handed me my bag, he tilted slightly to one side and had to brace himself with the wall. I pushed him toward the bed.

"Get comfortable and lie down."

He shot me a wicked grin which faded quickly. "You know, normally I would've loved to hear you say that. Right now, I think I'll just take your advice."

I went into the adjoining bathroom and stared in shock at my face. It was purple and swollen on one side with cuts and abrasions covering the rest. Breathing deeply, I reminded myself I was alive. The bruises would fade, and the abrasions would heal. I changed into a loose t-shirt and shorts before making my way back to the bedroom.

Griggs was lying on the bed, looking pale and sick. I turned around, walked back into the bathroom, and picked up the plastic trashcan. Returning to the bedroom, I placed it by his side of the bed.

He frowned. "What's that for?"

Using the bed for balance, I walked around to the other side. "In case you throw up."

"I'm not going to throw up."

I pulled back the covers and crawled under the sheets. I had no strength left. I laid my head down and closed my eyes.

"Why would I throw up?"

I huffed out a laugh. "Alex, you have the flu."

"No," he said. The bed moved. I opened my eyes to see

him trying to sit up. "I can't have the flu. I have to take care of you."

Reaching out, I pushed him back down. My hand slid down his arm to the end where I entwined my fingers with his. His hand closed around mine.

"We'll just have to take care of each other," I said as we drifted off to sleep.

###

ABOUT THE AUTHOR

B. L. Blair writes mystery/romance stories. Like most authors, she has been writing most of her life and has dozens of books started. She just needs the time to finish them.

She is the author of the Leah Norwood Mysteries and the Lost and Found Pets Mystery Novellas. She loves reading books, writing books, and traveling wherever and as often as time and money allows. She is currently working on her latest book set in Texas, where she lives with her family.

http://www.blblair.com
https://twitter.com/blblair100
https://www.facebook.com/blblair100
https://www.bookbub.com/authors/b-l-blair

By B. L. Blair:

Leah Norwood Mysteries
Dead in a Dumpster
Dead in a Park
Dead in a Pickup

Lost and Found Pets Mystery Novellas
The Lost Great Dane
The Lost Savannah
The Lost Spaniel
The Lost Macaw

Made in the USA
Middletown, DE
25 January 2019